Any Dream

Any Dream

JANET ROBERTSON

Fastnet Books

2013

Fastnet Books
227 Donnelly Street
Armidale, New South Wales, 2350
Australia

www.fastnetbooks.net

publishing@fastnetbooks.net

First published 2013

National Library of Australia
Cataloguing-in-Publication entry:

Robertson, Jane Rosemary Louise 1932 –
Any Dream

ISBN-13: 978-0-9871712-9-0
ISBN-10: 0987171291

Cover image by J. Rose Robertson

To the memory of Captain Allen Gardiner.

Contents

I

Chapter 1

In 1810 Allen Francis Gardiner joined the navy. In 1820 his best friend and neighbour, John Adam Gregory, was married. The two boys were born in the same year, 1794, and they had grown up on adjoining estates in the Shire of Goring near Oxford, England.

The Gardiner family lived at Coombe Lodge as had their ancestors for hundreds of years. Allen had several older brothers. The oldest would inherit Coombe Lodge, the next had joined the army, and the third had joined the church. Allen realised from an early age he would have to make a life for himself. And also at a very young age he knew he wanted to join the navy and serve his country. He idolised Admiral Nelson and his exploits, and although he knew life in the British navy would be hard, he started training his mind and his body for the tough years ahead.

On the other hand, his friend, John Gregory, came from a wealthy family who had made its fortune in sugar. When Britain lost its American colonies, the government determined that it would not lose its colonies in the West Indies, because the sugar grown in the Bahamas was vital to Britain's economy. John's father and grandfather owned several plantations. John's father, Sir William, had been to the West Indies several times as a young man. His first-born son William, John's older brother, was expected to do the same. Although William would inherit his father's title and much of his land, there was no necessity for John to pursue another career. He was an amiable, easy-going boy, who admired his friend's determination to make a life for himself. He had no aspirations of his own to leave the comfortable, pleasant life of the Gregory family. He was not jealous of his brother and seemed to share equally in his parents, Sir William and Lady Elizabeth, affections.

Every year the Gregory family went to London for the 'season'. Lady Elizabeth, a charming and beautiful woman, had maids, a housekeeper, and a cook to do her bidding. She managed to appear to be busy without actually doing very much at all. She chose the menus for the food they were to eat every day, chose the clothes she would wear, and, in a different sense, chose to be warm and friendly to everyone she met. Their estate, Melrose Park, ran like clockwork under Sir William's wise and comprehensive care.

When he turned fifteen, Allen went to sea as he had always intended. His hero Admiral Nelson had died at the Battle of Trafalgar in 1807. This made Allen even more determined to serve his country and make his family proud whatever the hardships to be faced. He was a thin but strong lad, with curly brown hair and a look of steely determination in his eyes.

John desperately missed his friend, Allen. The two boys had shared a tutor and shared the first fifteen years of their lives although they came from vastly different families.

By the time he went to sea, Allen's older brothers had left home, pursuing their own destinies. His mother was a gentle, soft-spoken and deeply religious woman. She spent her time helping those in trouble offering sympathy, food or money. John's mother, on the other hand, lived for the social season in London, loved pretty clothes and jewellery.

By the time Allen went to sea, John's older brother, William, was also enjoying the social season in London. He came home with stories of the pretty girls he met and the conquests he made. His parents encouraged him to marry someone with money or a title, or both.

William's exploits were of much less interest to John than the tales Allen brought home: tales of icebergs in the North Atlantic, and of the strange people and places in Africa and South America. Allen would be away for years at a time, returning home looking stronger, tanned and dedicated to the navy. Quickly rising through the ranks he was considered reliable, resourceful, and brave by his superiors.

John felt curiously envious of his friend's life. He knew he would never have the courage or the willpower to follow a similar path, but his own life seemed empty and meaningless. However, this all changed with the pending arrival of distant relations from Scotland, a father and daughter, Robbie and Sophia Stuart, who were cousins of William's. They were a sad pair, as Robbie's wife Amelia had died a month before their visit, leaving them lost and lonely.

'When they arrive,' Lady Elizabeth explained, 'we must be very kind and try to help them through their loss.'

'Yes, Mother. Of course, Mother,' her sons replied.

Robbie and Sophia arrived a few weeks later and after Lady Elizabeth made sure they were comfortably settled in their bedrooms, she brought them down to the drawing room to meet her family.

'Cousin Robbie, you know of course my husband, William, but you have not met my sons William and John.'

Robbie was a tall handsome man, but his face was strained and his eyes shadowed with grief. He had brown, wavy hair as did his daughter, Sophia. She was tiny, almost lost in the black gown she was wearing.

Elizabeth continued. 'We were so very sorry to hear of Amelia's illness. You must be lost without her.'

Robbie cleared his throat but couldn't speak, and Sophia's eyes filled with tears. She looked around hoping for some comfort, some easing of the pain, and when she caught John's eyes she clung to his look of sympathy and kindness.

He walked towards her and took her hands which were as cold as ice. 'I hope you will find some comfort and strength with us,' he murmured.

She looked up at him with tears still welling in her beautiful hazel eyes, and at that moment John felt his heart pounding – and he fell in love.

'Thank you, milady, and thank you cousin, you are very kind and generous.' Sophia murmured.

'Please Sophia, not so formal,' John replied. 'I am your cousin, and our home is your home as long as you need to be with us.'

In the weeks that followed John was delighted to see the pink return to Sophia's cheeks and the sparkle to her lovely hazel eyes. She had a soft lilting laugh and John did his utmost with his sense of fun just to hear it.

While Sir William and his older son showed the running of the estate to Robbie, Elizabeth and John had to keep Sophia entertained. John took her riding. She had an affinity with animals. She would talk, crooning really, to the horse she was riding and it always behaved calmly and gently, as if realising the person it were carrying needed special care. When she walked around the garden the dogs came up to her, wagging their tails, waiting for a pat or a kindly words. Even the cat, who thought he was the master of the house and walked past most people with haughty disdain, would jump into her lap when she sat talking to Lady Elizabeth or John, and purr contentedly.

'I've never seen Caesar take to a stranger so quickly,' Lady Elizabeth remarked in astonishment.

Sophia could play the piano, 'very badly' she would say, but John thought she was very talented. She admitted that she couldn't sew, and would sit struggling with a cross stitch while Lady Elizabeth plied her needle with extraordinary dexterity creating works of great beauty. Sophia pricked her fingers and was horrified when little drops of blood ruined her creations. Her eyes filled with tears.

'Never mind, my dear,' her hostess said, comfortingly. 'You have many other talents.'

'And you're so pretty', she thought to herself. She had noticed John gazing at Sophia with adoring eyes and was well pleased that something serious might develop between them.

After Sophia and her father's visit was over and they had returned to their home in Scotland, William and his father made a trip to the Bahamas to check their sugar plantations, leaving John in charge of the estate in England. He was busy but his heart wasn't in it. He was lonely and bored – in other words, lovesick. His mother noticed John's malaise. 'Is anything wrong?' she asked.

'Wrong? No, of course not,' was the reply.

'You miss Sophia, don't you?' she persisted.

'Well, yes, of course I miss her,' he stammered, face flushing.

'Are you serious about her, my dear?'

'Well I... well I...' He paused, 'Well yes, I love her, and would like to marry her.'

Lady Elizabeth smiled. 'She's a lovely girl. As soon as your father and brother come home you must go and visit her.'

'Yes I will, I will,' he agreed enthusiastically.

In the meantime, the young people wrote to each other. John tried to keep his letters from being too affectionate which would be inappropriate as he had not yet asked her father's permission to marry. Her letters were friendly and charming, and he read them over and over again. He hinted that he would like to visit Scotland as soon as his father and brother returned. This was greeted with much enthusiasm by Sophia part and John's depression turned to excitement at the thought of seeing her again. As soon as was practical upon his father's return to England, John rushed to Scotland and sought Sophie's father's permission to ask for her hand in marriage. This was willingly granted and, of course, Sophia consented at once when John proposed.

They were married the following year in late spring in Edinburgh. Sophia looked radiant and Robbie immensely proud of his lovely daughter.

Sophia had visited Melrose Park several times in the intervening months to supervise the refurbishment of one of the houses on the estate in which she and John would live after they were married. She had a flair for colour and her taste in furnishing was simple but elegant. Even Sir William and John's older brother grudgingly admitted that with her ideas the house that was to be their home looked remarkably comfortable and stylish.

John and Sophia began their married life with deep love and contentment. Sophia knew it was unlikely that John would ever inherit the title or the estate, but the family were so friendly and welcoming she believed it would never be a problem.

•

Allen Gardiner had also married. Since the age of fifteen he had sailed to many parts of the world, being away years at a time, interspersed with visits home. Over the nearly two decades of his naval service, he had become well respected for his courage and determination and his risen to the rank of Captain. He was tall and thin with a mop of curly hair, but a look of steely resolve in his eyes. This was tempered by flashes of humour and delight in telling amusing stories of his adventures.

He was pleased when John married Sophia, and soon after he himself married Julia Susanna Reade, who was both beautiful and intelligent. Descended from medieval kings and queens of England, kings of Scotland, and princes of Wales, while she boasted of her important ancestors, she was kind and sympathetic to people from all walks of life. Much to her mother-in-law's delight she was also deeply religious and the two would pray together for the unfortunate people Allen met in his travels, peoples who were subjugated by cruelty, superstition and greed.

Sophia and Julia became the best of friends and were thrilled when they both discovered they were pregnant. Julia gave birth to a daughter, also named Julia. She had lost a baby earlier in her marriage so she and Allen were delighted that the baby was healthy as was Julia herself.

Much to Sophia and John's delight, a few months later their son Adam was born. Lady Elizabeth and Sir William were proud grandparents for the first time. Secretly Lady Elizabeth was worried about their oldest son and heir, William, who showed no signs of settling down and spent more and more time in London, leaving his father and John to run the estate.

When, within a short time, Julia had a son, Allen, and Sophia a daughter, Amelia, both families felt blessed and very content with their lives. Although Allen still went to sea and was away for months at a time

Julia managed with the quiet determination to raise her children as Allen would wish and her faith sustained her.

When John first saw his daughter he gave a little gasp of surprise. Sophia had dark brown hair and so did her father but his little daughter's hair was red. Sophia checked at the expression on her husband's face.

'And she has green eyes. She's just like my mother.'

'Oh well, I didn't know, about the red hair, I mean,' John stumbled.

'How do you know she has green eyes?'

'She will have, because my mother did.' More hesitantly she went on. 'Do you think we could call her Amelia, after my mother?'

'Of course, Sophia. What a lovely idea.'

And so it was settled. The years slipped by in peace and harmony. Sophia was a little plumper than when they first met, but in John's eyes she seemed to grow more beautiful, as the time passed. He loved her sweet nature and her throaty chuckle when she was amused.

The only cloud on the horizon was John's brother William. He had finally become engaged to the Honourable Hermione Cavendish. She was both titled and an heiress, so Lady Elizabeth and Sir William were pleased with their son's choice. She wasn't really pretty but with her beautiful expensive clothes and sparkling jewellery she gave an attractive first impression. But she was cold and proud, treating her prospective mother-in-law and the rest of the family with disdain.

Although Sophia tried to be friendly and welcoming, she felt uncomfortable with Hermione's perfunctory politeness to her and her family. The wedding was a magnificent affair. Lady Elizabeth and Sir William were dazzled by their son's new wife.

Sophia kept her thoughts to herself, but John could see she was not impressed. 'You don't really like Hermione do you?'

Sophia flushed. John had never heard her speak ill of anyone but she had to be truthful. 'No, not really,' she admitted. 'She's cold and unkind,'

Sophia stumbled. 'When you take away the jewellery and the beautiful clothes I just don't think she's a very nice person.'

John agreed.

William and his new wife spent even more time in London enjoying the trappings of society. Most of Hermione's friends thought she had married beneath her. 'They make their money from sugar, you know,' they whispered, 'but, poor dear, she was getting desperate.'

A year later Hermione dutifully produced an heir, to be called William of course. 'I do hope she'll be a good mother.' Lady Elizabeth expressed her doubts about Hermione's character to her husband. She knew William had moved into a separate bedroom and wondered why.

The decision was all Hermione's. 'If you think I'm going through that again, you're very much mistaken,' Hermione had told her bewildered husband.)

'But he's your son, our son, surely that made it worthwhile?'

She gave her husband an icy stare.

Lady Elizabeth had become disillusioned with her new daughter-in-law over the previous year.

'I am still mistress of this house,' she complained to her husband. 'She countermands my orders and changes my menus. Who does she think she is?'

'She knows exactly who she is,' Sir William said wryly. 'She is the Honourable Hermione who happens to be wealthy. But don't worry, my dear, I'm sure she'll spend most of her time in London.'

'With a baby?' Lady Elizabeth protested.

'I think you'll find that you are expected to look after the child – with the help of nannies and maids, and cooks, and housekeepers. It shouldn't be too difficult. In fact I think you will probably enjoy it!'

Lady Elizabeth looked at her husband in stunned silence.

Young William was both spoilt and neglected and grew up a lonely little boy. The only thing he really enjoyed was being allowed to play with his cousins Adam and Amelia but this was not encouraged by his mother.

'Why doesn't Aunt Hermione like us?' Amelia once asked her mother.

'Well, she has her own friends who live in London, and she prefers to be with them,' Sophia tried to explain.

'But she doesn't often take William to London,' Amelia persisted. 'Why can't we do more things together? He must be lonely living with Grandma and Grandpapa and all those servants.'

Sophia sighed. 'I don't really know, Amelia. I can't understand it either.'

She gave her daughter a hug. With her long hair and green eyes, Amelia had grown to be the lovely girl that her mother had predicted when she was born. Her father adored her and would ask, 'How's my little Mel?' when he came in from a long day helping his father on the estate.

'My name's not Mel,' she would reply primly. 'It's Amelia.'

'Amelia? Really, someone should have told me.'

Amelia would always collapse in a fit of giggles. Then they would hug enjoying the daily joke.

Adam was a quiet, serious boy. He admired his father tremendously for his good humour and even temper. He also admired his work ethic as John worked hard, supervising the running of the estate. He knew what each of the men was doing or supposed to be doing. As his father grew older he had gradually taken over much of the control of the smooth running of Melrose Park.

'It's not fair Father, you do all the work, Uncle William is never here and yet he's going to inherit it all,' Adam pointed out.

John laughed. 'Don't worry about it, Adam. There's enough to go around for all the family. Uncle William will settle down when he has a family and I'm sure we'll all get on famously.'

'I still don't think it's fair. You work hard and Mother looks after the families that work for us. She's always taking things to their children and food if anyone is ill. I can't imagine Aunt Hermione ever doing that.'

'Well, I agree. Your Mother is an exceptional woman. Don't worry Adam everything will be all right.'

Somehow Adam didn't think so. He had not inherited his father's optimistic nature and could see there might be trouble ahead.

Chapter 2

Julia and Allen Gardiner had three children, Julia, Allen and Emma, and now she was pregnant again.

'Julia doesn't look well,' Sophia remarked to her husband. 'She looks so frail, I'm worried about her.'

Luckily Allen was at home for the time being and he was also worried about his wife. Julia always seemed to be busy caring for the children and for Allen's parents, and her kind devout Christian heart meant she never had time to look after herself. Allen noticed how weary she looked. Her eyes had lost their sparkle, and as her pregnancy progressed it was obvious that carrying the baby and all her duties left her exhausted.

'I wish you wouldn't try and do so much,' Allen entreated. 'Have a rest in the afternoon, let the maids do more for the children.'

'I love doing things for the children, and I'm perfectly alright. I just get a bit tired.'

Then tragedy struck. The new-born baby gave a few weak cries and stopped breathing. Julia lost a lot of blood and she could feel her life force gradually fading as she lay there.

'Can't you do something?' Allen, distraught, asked the doctor.

'I'm sorry Captain, I'm afraid there is nothing I can do.'

'Can I hold my baby?' Julia whispered. 'Isn't she beautiful?'

Allen nodded, his eyes filled with tears.

'I'll soon be with her in heaven.'

For the next two days Allen did not leave her side. He sat holding her hand, praying that God would not take his beautiful Julia from him. Occasionally her eyes would flicker and she would see her husband's anxious eyes.

'Don't leave me, Julia, please don't leave me. I need you, the children need you, I love you so much.'

She would smile, squeeze his hand and drift back into unconsciousness. Then in a lucid moment, she seemed disturbed and wanted to tell Allen something. He leant close. 'What is it my dear?'

'Allen, I want you to do something for me.'

'Anything, anything, my darling. I will do anything you want me to.'

She struggled to find the energy to say the words. 'We have talked many times about the sad lives of the people you have seen who have no hope and know not the love of Jesus Christ.'

'Yes, my dear, but don't tire yourself, just rest.'

'I must.' A little later she continued, 'You are a wonderful man, Allen, and I'm sure you could take the light that the knowledge of God's love can give to all people. Promise me.' She lay back exhausted.

'I promise, Julia.'

'God will go with you.'

'I promise Julia I will do all I can to help those people.'

She gave a glimmer of a smile. 'Allen, would you hold me?'

He cradled her gently in his arms until she finally stopped breathing, just like her daughter had only a few days before.

Grief-stricken, Allen went on holding her, praying that her faith would unite her with the baby girl.

Sophia and John were devastated by Julia and her baby's death and did all they could to comfort and help the bereaved father and his three children. John returned home a few weeks later obviously upset by Allen's plans.

'Sophia, do you know what Allen plans to do?'

Sophia nodded, Allen had told her of the promise he had made to his dying wife.

'The man's crazy with grief and he thinks he can go off and convert all the heathens in the world to Christianity. He must be stopped.'

Sophia knew of Allen's courage and determination and she didn't think anyone could stop him.

'He promised Julia when she was dying.'

'That's all very well, but he's a captain in the navy for goodness sake. What makes him think he can be a missionary?'

'With God's help.'

John groaned. 'You sounded like ...' he stopped abruptly.

'Julia?' Sophia bit her lip fighting back the tears.

'I'm sorry, I didn't mean... I just think he should stay at home and look after his children. They need him more than anyone. Somebody must stop him,' he muttered, obviously very distressed.

But there was no dissuading Allen and a few months later he set out for South Africa to keep his promise. He would spend the rest of his life trying to be the person Julia had believed him to be. Someone who could bring light to the darkness in which so many people lived.

●

While Allen was confronting the Zulus in South Africa, Sophia and John were having their own problems at Melrose Park. Sir William was becoming more and more frail and unable to cope with running the estate. John shouldered more and more responsibilities and his older brother spent more and more time in London with Hermione and young William. When they were home their son was not encouraged to spend time with his cousins, and Hermione openly snubbed the whole family.

Sophia's father had sent a young Scottish boy, Alex McDougall, to help John with chores around the house and garden and this led to a most unfortunate incident.

Amelia was out in the garden at the back of the house towards the orchard. She was playing with her dog Rusty, throwing a ball and running with the dog when he chased it. She tripped and fell forward flat on her face. The dog ran away in fright and at that moment Alex saw Amelia lying on the ground and ran forward to see if he could help. He knelt down beside her.

'Missy, Missy, are ye all right?'

There was no reply. He bent forward and touched her shoulder. 'Miss Amelia, are you all right?'

At that moment John spied them from the house and ran out shouting, 'What are you doing, boy? What have you done to Amelia?'

Alexander stood up. 'Nothing sir. I didna hurt her. She fell,' he stammered nervously.

John knelt beside Amelia. She did not move but she was breathing. 'What have you done, boy? If you've hurt my daughter, my god I'll ...'

At that moment the foreman, George, arrived.

'Get that boy out of my sight,' John yelled. 'He's hurt Amelia, get him out of here.' Quietly, John picked Amelia up while George dragged the boy now sobbing away. 'Lock him up,' John ordered sternly. 'I must look after my daughter.'

'Yes Mr John, don't worry, I'll deal with him.'

John carried his unconscious daughter inside and called his wife. 'Sophia come quickly, Amelia's been hurt.'

He laid her gently on the bed. A white-faced Sophia spoke to her gently, stroking her hand but there was no reply.

'What happened?' a tearful Sophia asked her husband.

'I don't know, that, that boy ... What shall we do?'

Sophia gently felt her daughter's arms and legs. 'She doesn't seem to have broken anything.' Then she noticed a lump appearing on Amelia's forehead. 'Oh look, she has bumped her head.'

John, concerned, leant over his daughter, felt her pulse and noted she was breathing normally.

'Just keep her warm, I'll go and fetch a doctor in the morning.'

'What happened?'

'I don't really know, we'll find out when she wakes up.'

'What if...?'

'She'll be alright, Sophia. Just keep that thought in your mind.'

Sophia nodded, but couldn't control the tears that were coursing down her cheeks.

During the night, Sophia, John and Adam took turns sitting with her. They held her hands and spoke gently to her, hoping her eyes would open.

'Bring your mother a cup of tea,' John said to Adam when the morning light seeped in to Amelia's bedroom.

'Of course, Dad. I'll bring you one too.'

'Amelia, can you hear me, darling?' Sophia urged gently.

'Wake up little Mel, wake up,' her father insisted.

The girl's eyes flickered, then opened. 'Mother? Father? What happened? Where am I?'

'You're in your bed, darling. You fell over and bumped your head.'

'Yes, it hurts.'

'Do you remember why you fell over?' her father asked.

'No, no, I can't remember. Oh! my head hurts.'

John murmured to Sophia, 'I think I'll ride into Oxford and ask Dr Little to come and examine her, make sure everything is all right.'

Adam approached with cups of tea. 'Well sister, I'm glad you've woken up. Gave us quite a scare.'

'Scare? Why? When did I fall over?'

'Yesterday my darling, but don't worry, your father is going to fetch a doctor. Now you must rest.'

Sophia bathed Amelia's face with a cool washer. 'My head hurts,' Amelia muttered. 'Try and get some sleep. I'll be here, I won't leave you,'

Sophia said.

'Thank you, mother.' Amelia closed her eyes and drifted off to sleep again.

The doctor advised that she stay in bed for a few days. 'I'm sure there's no permanent damage,' he told her worried parents, 'But if the headaches get any worse let me know straight away.'

Sophia hovered over her daughter for several days, spoiling her with love and attention. Finally Amelia announced she was sick of being in bed and she wanted to get up and get some fresh air. The headaches finally went away but Amelia still had no idea what had made her fall.

'Did you see anyone else when you went out in the garden?' John asked diplomatically.

'No, no-one. Why should I see anyone?'

'No reason,' John replied calmly. He had told his foreman George to send the Scottish boy back to Scotland and as far as anyone knew that is what happened to him. John and Sophia were careful not to mention his name. If Amelia couldn't remember seeing him it was probably best for everyone to forget the incident.

Amelia learned not to complain about her intermittent headaches in order not to worry her mother.

Eventually, Allen returned from South Africa. His children, Julia, Allen and Emma were overjoyed to see him, as he was to see them.

'I hope Allen has got these missionary ideas out of his system,' John confided to Sophia.

'Yes, he needs to be with his children, to stay at home and give them a proper life.'

If they thought this is what Allen would do, they were both wrong. A few months later Allen announced he was returning to South Africa with his children and a new wife. He had married Elizabeth, the daughter of a local parson. John and Sophia had been appalled.

'I thought he loved Julia so much that he ... I can't understand him,' Sophia complained.

'I suppose he thinks the children need a mother. She seems a good woman.' John had sought to explain Allen's actions.

'I suppose she is, but when I think of Julia ...' Sophia began to cry. 'He's different. Don't you think he's different?'

'Well, he's thinner than ever, he looks weary, there's something about his eyes, but he's just as brave as I remember him.'

Sophia wondered if you could be *too* brave.

Allen explained his desire to return to South Africa was that he wanted to create a settlement in Natal on the land that the Zulu chief Dingarn had given him and he felt it was his duty to return with his family to oversee the building of the new settlement. The children accepted their new mother, and excitedly looked forward to the trip. It would be a great adventure for them after their years of loneliness without their beautiful mother and their father.

'You should come out there too,' Allen suggested to John, 'I can't see much of a future for you here.'

John shook his head. 'I must stay here while my mother and father are still alive, after that, I don't know.'

Allen and his family intended to settle in the Berza, a spot high on the hill above the malaria-infested coastline of Natal. The settlement was called Durban after the governor of South Africa.

Just before they arrived in Natal, tragedy struck. Julia, who had been poorly for most of the trip, became gravely ill and died just before they reached their destination. She was the first white child to be buried in Durban. Who could know the agony it must have been for Allen to lose another Julia?

Allen tried to explain to heartbroken Allen and Emma that it was God's will.

'If your God's so wonderful, why did he let her die?' Allen asked his father. The pain and grief in his voice was heartbreaking.

Allen replied gently. 'We don't always know what God's plans are, but we must accept them.'

'Well I'm not going to,' Allen yelled. 'I don't like your God!'

'Hush, children.' Their stepmother put her arms around them. 'We must all be strong and brave. Come with me, it's nearly tea time.'

They moved to the Berza, on the hills away from the malaria-infested coast. Allen set about establishing the small town and organising religious services. The children, at first deeply upset by their sister's death, began to enjoy the strange country with its different peoples, warmer climate and less regimented life.

However, the uneasy situation with the Zulus went from bad to worse. A group of Boers thought they might acquire some land in the same way Captain Allen had done – by visiting Dingarn. However, they were all massacred and it became clear that the Gardiner family were not safe living in Durban and so they returned to England.

John and Sophia had been deeply distressed by the news of little Julia's death and hoped that they would now stay in England and lead a normal, peaceful life. But this was not to be.

Instead of settling down in England, Allen took his wife and children on a trip sailing round the world trying to find a worthy place where he could spread his message of Christian love. In the end he decided on South America and with his wife and children, journeyed by coach from Buenos Aires across the Pampas and the Andes to Chile. This was a dangerous undertaking. There were groups of hostile Indians, and before attempting to cross the mountains, he was told the passes were still blocked by snow. He persisted and they came through safely. After realising that Roman Catholics had founded missions in most areas of South America he returned to England. Here he founded the South American Missionary Society and travelled round Great Britain raising money for an expedition he had believed was his destiny. It was to take the Christian message to the natives of Tierra del Fuego — the Land of Fire. He knew that no Roman Catholics had attempted to reach this small island in the southern region of South America. It was viewed by some as the uttermost end of the earth but nothing daunted Allen. He raised enough men for the trip, persuaded five other men to accompany him and set out for the Falkland Islands. This time he left his long suffering wife and children behind.

But on arriving in Tierra del Fuego, disaster struck. Their boat was wrecked and storms washed away their meagre provisions. A relief ship took too long to arrive and Allen and his men, having been unable to make contact with the hostile natives, slowly starved to death.

When the news eventually arrived in England, John held his head in his hands. 'What a waste. I can't believe it. Allen was always so well organised, how could things have gone so wrong?'

'When you travel to the ends of the earth things are bound to go wrong,' Sophia tried to explain. 'He was just following his dream.'

'Dream? Following his dream? More like a nightmare I should think.'

'Don't say that John,' Sophia was distressed by her husband's attitude.

'I can't help it, he should have been home with his wife and children.'

'Allen just wasn't that sort of person,' Sophia said gently. 'He had to have a challenge, needed to feel he was making a difference in the world.'

'I know, I know, but it's a terrible waste. He was such a good friend.

I don't know how I'll manage without him,' John said. 'Or my father,' he added.

John's father had died only a few months before he heard of Allen's death. His brother was now Sir William, owner of Melrose Park, the estates in Jamaica, and even the house in which John and his family lived. The idea that there would always be enough for all the family after his parents' death had not taken into consideration the nature of William's wife, Lady Hermione.

John felt his family's position was becoming more vulnerable but knew that while his mother was alive there would be an uneasy truce between the two families.

As the months went by Lady Elizabeth faded before their eyes. John and Sophia begged her to come and live with them.

'I will not be pushed out of my home.' She was determined Hermione's unkind attitude would not make her leave.

'I have lived here since I was married and I will live here until I die.'

'But we would love to have you live with us,' Sophia pleaded. 'We all love you.'

'I know dear, you're very kind,' Lady Elizabeth was determined. The strain of her husband's death and Hermione's cold selfishness affected Lady Elizabeth's health. She suffered a heart attack and died a year after her husband passed away.

John and Sophia felt as if life as they had known it would not last much longer. Grieving for his parents and the loss of Allen, John became silent and morose. Sophia, Adam, and Amelia tried to raise his spirits but they all knew he was desperately worried.

Work on the estate seemed to proceed as usual with John overseeing the work and William and Hermione travelling to London. John was thankful for the money his father had given him before he died as he felt sure he would need it and fairly soon.

One day William sent a message to John asking him to come to the manor as soon as possible as he had some business to discuss with him. John's heart sank.

'This is it,' he said to Sophia, as he put on his coat. It was a cold winter's morning and Sophia's smile and hug did not make him feel any warmer.

'You don't know that.'

'I'm afraid I do.'

II

Chapter 3

Demelza yawned and then groaned. She had opened her eyes to see the spring sunshine streaming into her bedroom. She had slept in.

Quickly she jumped out of bed, threw on her underclothes then her long blue dress. After brushing her hair she pulled it back and tied it with a ribbon. As she walked along the passage she pulled on a woollen jacket. Then out on the veranda and into the kitchen. Here her brother Johnny was toasting bread over an open fire and her mother was stirring something on the fuel stove.

'Well, little sister,' her brother greeted her, 'a little late, aren't we?'

'Don't be silly, Johnny,' their mother disagreed. 'Demelza can sleep a little late on Sunday morning if she wants to. Here's your porridge, Demelza.'

'Thank you, mother.'

After sprinkling her porridge with sugar and pouring cream on it Demelza silently ate her breakfast.

'You'll get fat eating all that sugar and cream,' Johnny teased.

'No I won't. I don't get fat,' she said, 'because I work so hard.'

Johnny roared with laughter. 'Doing what?' he asked.

'Now, now, children, enough of that nonsense.' Milly smiled. Her children brought her so much joy. She thanked God for them and her husband Jack every day.

Jack came in and slammed the back door. He warmed his hands by the roaring fire. He was tall, fair-haired and blue-eyed, with a face weathered by sunny New England summers and cold New England winters.

'Cuppa?' Milly asked.

'Yes please. So what are the plans for today?'

'It's Sunday, that means you have a spell,' his wife said firmly.

Johnny laughed. 'And that means we do some gardening.'

Milly nodded, 'Well, there are a few things I need someone to help with.'

Milly loved her garden; it was a wonderful relaxation from cooking and housework.

'But it's cold outside,' Demelza protested.

'Rubbish, the sun's shining. It's going to be a lovely day.'

'Well, I'm very happy here.' Johnny yawned. 'I think I'll just stay by the fire.'

The kitchen was warm and cosy. It was a hot large room and the walls were dingy from years of smoke from the open fire and the fuel stove. There was a door that led to the verandah, bedrooms, and lounge room. A window faced south and there was a table on which there was a basin and jug for washing dishes, and enough space for Milly and Demelza to prepare meals and where the family had breakfast. The door next to the open fire led to the back veranda and the dining room. Beyond the back porch in a small paddock was the long drop – the lavatory. To the right of the porch, a laundry, to the left a few fruit trees and vegetable garden down past the clothes line. Because houses were built from timber, kitchens were often totally separate from the rest of the house in case of fire. This was also the reason the laundry was banished to the next paddock. On wash day the copper was lit, the men's work clothes scrubbed and boiled and rinsed and rung by hand. It was hard work. To iron the clothes, heavy little 'Mrs Potts' irons were heated on the stove and replaced frequently as they cooled. The floors were mopped and polished every week and Milly and Jack's house was always spotless. It was hard work but Milly was a sturdy little woman and never complained. Demelza did her best to help and everyone knew her great love was her garden. Jack grew the fruit and vegies and Milly grew the flowers. She liked to have a few flowers on the dining table and in the bedrooms but the New England winters were cold, there were frosts, the occasional fall of snow and cold winds sweeping in from the Antarctic, so flowers were not always available.

Milly's greatest joy was a little magnolia tree that was growing in the front garden. Every day she would go out and have a little chat to it, encourage it to grow big and strong.

Johnny was fair like his father, but Demelza had beautiful long red hair and green eyes. When Jack first saw his baby daughter Milly laughed at the look of astonishment on his face.

'Is she really ours?' he asked.

Milly explained, 'My mother had red hair and green eyes.' A wave of sadness crossed her face. 'Not that I ever saw her hair or her eyes. You know she died when I was born. I have my grandmother's colouring.'

Jack patted her hand. He knew she had had a rather sad and lonely childhood. She had not known her mother or her father, but was cared for by her grandmother Sophia, and her aunt Caroline and uncle Adam Gregory. They had been loving and kind but couldn't quite take the place of the mother and father she had never known. As Demelza grew older, Adam told Milly she was the image of the mother Milly had never known and this gave her some comfort. Milly was named Amelia after her mother, but because of her tragic death, her grandmother and father had always called her Milly.

•

Milly's grandparents, Sophia and John Gregory, her mother Amelia and Uncle Adam had come to Australia in 1852. This was because John's older brother William had inherited the family's estates, leaving John with only a small amount of money. They had been persuaded by friends to venture into the unknown, to migrate across to the other side of the world. Milly often thought how brave they must have been. Sophia and John had their doubts at first, thinking they were too old for such an adventure. Amelia and Adam were enthusiastic, full of wide-eyed wonder at the thought of living in a new country where the sun always shone, or so they were led to believe.

Adam was the driving force behind the expedition. He was bitter and angry that after all his father's years of hard work the estates had gone to his wastrel uncle and his unpleasant wife and snobbish son. He was entirely sick of England's class-ridden society and longed for the country where life would be free and fair. Even the convicts who have served their time can make a better life for themselves than the poor people in England who can never rise above the station into which they were born he was told.

His father was less impressed. 'That's just a dream.'

'It's not a dream, it's real,' Adam replied. 'Come on, father, let's try it, we can always come back if things don't work out.'

'We'll see....'

Seeing the light in his son's eyes and the enthusiasm in his voice when the word New South Wales was mentioned, John gradually allowed himself to be convinced.

'What do you think, Sophia?' he asked.

'If we are all together we can live happily anywhere.'

And so the die was cast; Amelia and Adam were ecstatic.

'What an adventure! Uncle William can have silly old estates, we're going to New South Wales!'

The voyage to Sydney was long and tedious. After overcoming sea-sickness, some storms and endless days of rain and wind they wondered if their dream would ever become a reality.

Finally they arrived in Sydney and the shop moored in the vast harbour. As Sophia looked out at the sights on land her heart sank. It looked so different, the colours were different, the skies were brighter, it seemed unutterably strange.

'Come on mother, isn't this great? We are here at last!' Adam exalted.

'Thank God for that,' John murmured. 'At last we can get off this blasted ship!'

John organised their luggage to be taken ashore and they slowly made their way down and stood on Australian soil, but it went up and down underneath their feet. After months at sea it would take a few days to be accustomed to solid ground.

'I feel giddy,' Amelia complained.

'Come on, Sis, don't tell me you're drunk at this hour of the day!' Adam teased.

'Certainly not,' she snapped, 'I've never been drunk in my life. Not like some people I know!'

They settled into a boarding house in Sydney town while John made enquiries about their next destination. He had letters of introduction to several well-known Sydney identities and Adam had long conversations with them about where they would go and what they would do with the money John's father had given them.

While John and Adam had their business discussions, Sophia and Amelia investigated Sydney town. To Sophia it was strange and daunting; to Amelia it was exciting and wonderful. Everywhere they went Amelia drew admiring glances with her long red hair, slim figure, her lively expression and her eyes sparkling. She was a beautiful young woman. Sophia felt a little uneasy at some of the looks that came their way. She would be glad when they were settled in their new home – wherever that might be.

John felt the same unease about their future abode. His heart was heavy with the knowledge that the decision he made would affect the rest of their lives.

One night he said to Sophia, 'I do wish Allen was here, just to see his face and hear his voice would be a great comfort to me.'

Although he had seen little of his friend over the last few years of his life, he never forgot the great friendship they had shared as boys and young men. John sighed, 'I guess he never found his dream.'

'We don't know that,' Sophia disagreed.

'You mean dying of starvation in a land no-one has ever heard of, trying to help natives who didn't even want him there was fulfilling his promise to Julia?' John sounded quite agitated.

She tried to sound comforting. 'He will go down in history as a brave and exceptional human being. I'm sure he'll be remembered as a saint many years from now.'

'What good is history to his wife and children? I'm sure they'd rather have a husband and father than a dead saint!'

'Try not to worry.' Sophia was concerned at her husband's agitation. 'We just have to have faith that everything is going to be alright.'

She put her arms around her husband.

'Sophia, what would I do without you, you are so brave and kind...'

'Hush, just believe in our love, and God's love, and Allen's love, because he does still love you.'

Tears came to John's eyes but the pain and torment in his heart was eased as he felt the love and warmth of Sophia's body wrapping him in security and optimism.

'Of course, of course my darling Sophia, we are going to make the right decisions. I know we are.'

They chose the Hunter Valley as the best location for their future home. Being one hundred miles north of Sydney, the quickest and easiest way to get there was to sail by boat from Sydney to Morpeth. With the Hunter River flowing through the hills and plains the fertile land was suitable for farming and grazing. John and Adam initially made two trips to the region. They were shown around the district making important decisions on the climate, soil, and price of the land. They needed an area large enough from which they could make a living, but within their financial boundaries. Sophia and Amelia joined them on their third expedition. They had seen several suitable blocks but were told one of them was too close to the river which flooded from time to time. Adam had his heart set on another place further from the river but not too far from the main town of Maitland.

'What do you think mother? I think this would be perfect,' Adam enthused.

'Well, I don't know,' Sophia murmured. She was feeling daunted by the strange landscape, the strange trees, the strange colours.

'It's… it's so different,' Sophia stumbled.

Adam laughed, 'Of course it's different, this is New South Wales. I think it's wonderful.'

Sophia looked pleadingly at John. 'Can we afford it?' she asked.

'Yes, yes, and there'll be enough to build us a lovely home. We can plan it all ourselves.'

'That would be fun, mother,' Amelia suggested, noticing her mother's hesitation.

'And we can do it all ourselves,' Adam went on, 'we don't have to ask anyone's permission.' John was silent. 'Come on father, you know this is the best land that we've looked at.'

'Yes, yes I agree.' John hesitatingly replied.

Sophia wondered at her husband's reticence. Could it be that for once he didn't have to ask his father or his brother and it felt strange?

Seeing the smiling faces of his children, however, John tried to relish the thought that it would be his home, his land and his family's future.

'It's settled then, this is it,' he said firmly.

After making all the arrangements and paying a deposit, the family returned to Sydney in a glow of optimism and anticipation of a bright future.

There were many weary months while they waited for their house to be built and John and Adam found out as much as they could about making a living in the Hunter Valley.

Sometimes at night Sophia ached with homesickness for her beloved England and Scotland. She couldn't get used to the too-bright blue skies, the different colour of the hills, the grass and the trees. The relentless dingy colour of the endless gum trees really upset her. She longed for the bright colours and flowers of England but tried not to let her family see her distress.

One day Adam said to her, 'You know father seems so much happier without Grandpa or Uncle William telling him what to do.'

'I know,' agreed Sophia, 'He just has you telling him what to do.' Adam laughed. At least his mother had not lost her sense of humour. 'No problem there,' he said airily.

'He looks so tired, I worry about him,' Sophia continued, 'you will make sure he doesn't do too much?'

'Of course mother, don't worry.'

Sophia was unpleasantly surprised by the heat of the long summer days. Under instructions from their architect they built their house with verandas and breeze ways. The idea was to keep the sun's rays out of the house, not to welcome them as they had in England. Sophia felt lethargic in the midday heat and couldn't sleep at night.

Adam and Amelia revelled in the bright sunny days but Amelia was careful to wear a large hat and long-sleeved shirts to protect her fair skin from getting burnt. Although they were close to a creek that fed into the Hunter River they were told to build rain water tanks.

'You never know when we'll get a dry spell,' one of the builders told them. 'Sometimes it can go weeks without rain, or even months. Some places in this country it doesn't rain for years,' he added enigmatically.

'Really? I can't believe that.' Sophia thought he was joking.

John and Adam went about the serious business of buying stock for their property. They bought sheep but these were to produce wool not the meat that had been their income at Melrose Park. They acquired cows, and John taught Adam how to milk. Hens were a must to supply them with eggs, and a few pigs that could be killed for special occasions.

They hired a young man to help with the heavy work - fences had to be built and the sheep needed dosing for worms and treated for fly strike. There were flies, mosquitoes, spiders and snakes. There was much to learn about their new country.

Adam and Amelia enjoyed the freer, friendlier attitude of the people they met.

'I think it's grand,' Adam told his father. 'That class-ridden nonsense we had to put up with – I'm glad it's different here.'

John agreed but as the months went by he felt more and more tired and less able to cope with the many problems that required his decisions.

They began to make friends with the neighbours; the little town of Maitland was sufficient for the purchase of their daily requirements. Occasionally they made the trip to Sydney if something special was needed.

After nearly two years, they had come to feel more at home in their drastically altered surroundings, but at the same time Sophia became more and more worried about her husband's health.

'Please make sure your father doesn't do any heavy work,' she admonished Adam. 'He looks so tired these days.'

'Don't worry, I'll look after him,' Adam replied. But he was just as worried himself.

One day they rode out to check on the sheep in a paddock further from the house. John dismounted to open a gate. To his horror Adam saw his father gasp, clutch his chest and fall, to lie crumpled on the ground.

'Father, father, are you alright?' He rushed and knelt by his father but John had stopped breathing. 'Oh my God, oh my God, what will I do?'

In the distance Sophia saw Adam riding very slowly with his father in his arms and leading his father's horse.

She called Amelia and they ran to meet the approaching figures. 'John?' she asked.

Adam shook his head.

'Oh my darling, my poor darling.' Tears flowed down her cheeks.

The chaos of the next few days was unbearable. Sophia seemed lost in a private, painful world where no-one could reach her.

'We shouldn't have come. Why did we come?' she asked Adam and Amelia. 'We should have stayed in England where we belonged. I hate this place,' she sobbed. 'I want to go home. I don't belong here. None of us do.'

Amelia tried to comfort her but to no avail.

Friends and neighbours came to their aid. The men advised Adam and the women comforted Sophia and Amelia – except for one man who seemed more interested in comforting Amelia than advising Adam. He was Dominic Raymond, their closest neighbour. He owned a property close to the Hunter River. Tall, dark, and good-looking, after inheriting some money from his grandfather he had settled in the colony, intrigued by the opportunities a place like New South Wales offered, five years, before the arrival of the Gregory family. Self-reliant and adventurous, he had arrived in the Hunter Valley after visiting Canada, New Zealand and Western Australia. When he first saw Amelia he thought how beautiful she was, but how she was sweet with it and had a puckish sense of humour that made him laugh. Before her father's death he had admired her from afar, but now he saw the opportunity for a closer relationship.

He started dropping in every few days to see if there was anything the family needed. He invited them all to dinner. Seeing the surprised expression on Sophia's face, Dominic laughed. 'I do have a cook and a housekeeper. I assure you the dinner should be more than palatable.'

Sophia felt confused. 'I'm so sorry. We would love to come to dinner.' Her face lit up and she smiled. Adam and Amelia felt their sadness lifting a little.

Dominic made a charming host and Amelia and Sophia were impressed by his house, its furnishings, and even his servants.

'He must have a lot of money,' Adam remarked after they returned home.

'Yes, I expect so,' his mother agreed. 'But he isn't full of himself, or arrogant, he just seems like a very nice person.'

Amelia silently agreed and her heart quickened as she thought of the handsome Dominic.

The romance blossomed, lifting the family out of the despair they had felt after John's death.

Adam took over the role of the man of the family, and was glad when he could see his mother's improved spirits.

'You know, mother,' he said to her, 'you can't really blame Australia for what happened to father. The death of his mother and father and the loss of his friend, Allen Gardiner, disturbed him, and on top of that Uncle William's horrible behaviour was a terrible blow.'

Sophia nodded, she knew this all to be true.

'Think how much worse things would have been if father had died when we were still in England. Then we would have really faced disaster. Here, we have a lovely home, a good property from which we make a comfortable living, and good friends.'

'Yes, you are right, Adam dear, it's just, it's just...' Tears came to Sophia's eyes. 'I'm just a silly old thing. I know this is a good place to live.'

Adam hugged his mother. 'You're not silly at all, especially when you smile, then you are beautiful.'

She smiled.

Amelia walked round in a haze of happiness. Dominic was so sweet, so kind, so handsome, so everything. They were married in the late spring. Amelia looked beautiful and happy; Sophia was extremely proud of both her children. Adam gave the bride away and Caroline Harris, Amelia's best friend, was bridesmaid. In turn she hoped that she would be more than a friend to Adam. The four of them seemed blessed with a bright future and much happiness in store.

Sophia too beamed with pleasure, hoping that their fortunes would hold nothing but joy and happiness, but the bubble burst as sadness follows joy with monotonous regularity.

A few months after they were married Amelia realised she was pregnant. Everyone was delighted and Amelia glowed with health and happiness. She knew her doting husband would be a wonderful father – she was sure of it.

Having got through her early pregnancy without too many problems, Amelia was proud of her swelling stomach and so excited when she felt the baby's first kicks. She and her mother made beautiful baby clothes and prepared one of the bedrooms to be a nursery.

Adam and Caroline Marwick were married three months before Amelia's baby was due and Sophia welcomed her new daughter-in-law with open arms, deferring to her with decisions in running the house.

'But this is your home,' Caroline protested. 'You don't need to ask me about anything.'

Remembering the cruel way John's sister-in-law had treated his mother, Sophia felt warmth and comfort in the younger woman's response.

'But I like to hear your hopes and opinions. Adam is a lucky man to have such a thoughtful wife.'

'I do hope it's a little girl,' Amelia confessed a few weeks before her baby was due. Sophia seemed surprised; she was sure Dominic longed for a son and heir as most men did, but she agreed with Amelia.

'Daughters are very special,' she confided. 'But I'm sure we'll all love a boy or girl.'

All went well until Amelia went into labour. The pains were strong and exhausting, but the baby just did not seem to want to be born. Sophia and Caroline sat with Dominic and grew more and more agitated.

'Isn't it taking too long?' he asked his mother-in-law.

'Don't worry, Dominic, sometimes the birth does take a long time. It's her first baby after all. I'm sure everything will be alright.' Sophia sounded more confident than she felt.

Dominic paced up and down. 'I hope that doctor knows what he's doing.' Adam arrived and suggested they go for a walk to fill in time. 'No, no, I can't leave, Amelia might need me.'

Finally they heard a baby cry. A few minutes later the doctor approached. 'You have a beautiful baby girl,' he said to Dominic.

They all embraced each other – what wonderful news. Then Sophia noticed a strange look on the doctor's face.

'You must come and be with your wife, and you too Mrs Gregory. Come at once.'

When they entered the room, Amelia was lying still, too still, but her eyes were open.

'We have a little girl,' she whispered.

Sophia looked anxiously at the doctor. 'What is wrong?' she whispered.

He took her aside. 'I'm sorry, Mrs Gregory, but I'm afraid I cannot save your daughter.'

Sophia rushed to the side of the bed. 'Amelia, Amelia darling. You have the little girl you wished for.'

Amelia's eyes flickered and she gave a little smile. Then she closed her eyes forever. Dominic shouted at the doctor, 'What is wrong with my wife? What has happened?'

The doctor shook his head. 'The labour took too long. Something has happened. We're not quite sure...'

'Not sure? Amelia? Amelia?' There was no reply.

Dominic leant over and kissed her lips. They were cold.

No-one had taken any notice of the baby, still crying in the nurse's arms.

'Would you like to hold your daughter?' the nurse asked. He brushed her aside.

'No, I just want my wife.' He knelt beside the bed, his shoulders shaking with emotion.

Sophia took the baby. She was beautiful with brown hair and a dear little face.

Sophia looked at Caroline, unable to believe what had just happened. She had a granddaughter but her beautiful daughter was gone. She felt faint with the shock and Caroline sat her in a chair, giving the baby back to the nurse.

'What shall we do?' she gasped. 'My God, what are we going to do?'

It was Caroline who made arrangements for a wet nurse and a permanent nanny for the baby. And it was Adam who made the funeral arrangements. Dominic had gone into shock and shut himself in his room and wouldn't speak to anyone.

In time, Caroline tried to find out from the doctor the reason for her sister-in-law's sudden death.

'It seems the strain of labour made a clot which burst and bled into her brain. Do you know if she had a fall or hurt her head lately?'

Caroline shook her head but later asked Sophia who was cuddling the poor little motherless baby.

Then Sophia remembered. 'Of course, she did have a fall, before we left England. It was that, that boy's fault. It is he who killed my daughter.'

Adam tried to comfort his hysterical mother. 'You mustn't believe that, you really mustn't. Alex cannot be blamed. We don't even know if he had anything to do with Amelia's fall. Besides the doctor wasn't positive that a fall caused her death.' His voice trailed away. 'Now mother, you must pull yourself together. This little baby needs you. You must love her and look after her. It doesn't look like her father is going to be much use.'

'Yes, of course, Amelia's baby. Don't worry I shall take care of her.'

Sophia tried to get Dominic to take some interest in the baby but he could barely bring himself to look at her.

'What would you like to name her? How about Amelia?'

'Yes, yes, whatever you like.'

'I don't think that's a very good idea,' Adam said to his mother later. 'The name will just remind us of our lovely Amelia every time we say it.'

'We could call her Milly,' Caroline suggested. 'That's short for Amelia.'

When Sophia suggested this to Dominic he simply said, 'Yes, yes whatever you like.'

'It's just as well Milly doesn't have red hair,' Caroline said to Adam. 'Actually I think she looks like your mother.'

'Do you? Yes, perhaps she does.'

Sophia stayed on with Dominic and Milly, seeing to the baby's care and trying to get Dominic to recover from his grief and take an interest in his daughter. She found a courage she did not know she possessed and bravely faced her daily tasks even though she thought life without her darling beautiful Amelia was going to seem empty and meaningless.

Adam and Caroline tried to persuade Sophia to bring the baby to be with them until Dominic regained his interest in life. Sophia refused, saying she was going to encourage Dominic to love his daughter.

'He still doesn't show any signs of that?' Caroline asked.

Sophia shook her head sadly. 'He gave her a peck on her forehead at bedtime and that's about it. I just wish he realised Amelia left him a gift, a lovely little girl, someone he can love and who will love him.'

'I wouldn't mention the Scottish lad you thought might have hurt Amelia,' Adam advised.

'Why not?'

'Because we have no proof he had anything to do with Amelia's accident. She did not remember seeing him or anything about him.'

'I don't agree, I think he should be told.'

'The state that man is in, he would likely rush to Scotland, looking for him and end up...' He paused, 'hurting him, even killing him.'

Sophia looked startled. 'I hadn't thought of that, perhaps you're right.'

'Just let him believe she fell as a child, and we don't even know that is the reason why she died.'

'Do you know what happened to that boy?'

Adam shook his head. 'Father handled it. I don't know what happened to him.'

'Then Dominic will think it was my fault for not looking after her or Milly's fault for just being born!'

'You can tell Milly later, when she's old enough to understand about your suspicions. I strongly advise you not to mention it now.'

'Then Milly will think it was her fault that her mother died.'

'We won't ever let her think that,' Caroline said soothingly. 'We will just make sure she knows we all love her and her father too.'

•

Milly was a good baby, and was developing into a very pretty child. She did indeed look more like her grandmother than anyone else in the family. She rarely cried and seeing her grow and flourish eased the pain in Sophia's heart over the death of her daughter.

But the hoped-for burgeoning of Dominic's love for his child was not to be. When Milly was six-months-old, Dominic received a letter from his family asking that he return to England immediately because his father was very ill. Dominic, looking even more worried than usual, came to Sophia still holding the letter in his hand.

'I have had bad news from my family. I must return to England immediately. Can you look after the baby?'

'Of course I will, but must you go? Your daughter needs you.'

'I must. I'll engage a manager to run this place, and would appreciate it if Adam could keep his eye on things.'

Sophia was devastated.

'Don't worry, mother,' Adam told her. You and Milly and the nurse will be as welcome to live with us until he gets back.' If he gets back, he thought to himself.

33

And so it was arranged. In a matter of weeks Dominic had gone.

For a few months he wrote regularly, sending money for Milly's expenses. Then he arranged with Adam for money to be paid from the income of his property. His father died and still there was no sign of his return.

Milly had her first birthday but there was no greeting from her father.

'I suppose he can only remember that it was the day his wife died.' Sophia tried to forgive his neglect.

By this time Adam and Caroline had a child of their own, a son, David. It had been an anxious time, but Caroline and the baby flourished. Adam decided to build more rooms on to their home to accommodate his expanding family.

'But Milly and I will return to Dominic's house as soon as he comes back,' Sophia protested.

'No matter, we need a larger house anyway,' Adam replied, keeping his thoughts about his brother-in-law to himself.

Then the blow fell.

Sophia received a letter from Dominic's lawyer in England. He explained that Mr Raymond would not be returning to Australia. Income from the property next door to the Gregory's was to be used for Milly's education and other needs, and at the age of twenty-one the property would be made over to her unconditionally.

'Mother, what is it?' Adam asked, seeing his mother's face flush then go deathly pale.

Sophia struggled for words. 'He, he's not coming back, not ever,' and the tears flowed down her cheeks.

'I didn't think he would,' Adam said.

'How can he leave his lovely little daughter and never want to see her?'

'I think he loved Amelia so much,' Caroline said gently, 'that when she died it shattered his existence. Something snapped in his heart, leaving him unable to love his daughter. She is better off with you, Mother. And you know we all love her and will treat her as our own.'

'The poor little motherless, fatherless thing,' Sophia sobbed. 'But she will have a doting grandmother, aunt and cousins.' Caroline was pregnant again. In due time, she gave birth to a daughter she and Adam named Sophie, after Adam's mother.

•

Milly grew to be a rather quiet and self-contained child, but she could be obstinate and have flashes of temper that seemed to come out of nowhere.

'Keep away from Milly when she gets that look in her eyes,' David warned his sister Sophie.

But Milly did feel a sense of loss. There was a black hole in her soul she did not visit often, but it was there.

Over all Milly, Sophie and David had a happy childhood. The girls learned to cook, sew and to play the piano, necessities in young ladies at the time. David learnt from his father how to run a property, both the care of the stock, and the attention to financial matters required for them all to have a comfortable life. Milly, however, took little interest in the property that was to be hers some day. There seemed to be something tainted about it, the thought that her father could make up for years of neglect by giving her a property. Eventually Sophia learned that he had married again and had more children, but she was reluctant to worry Milly with this information.

Sophia kept a serene eye on the whole family as her son and his wife moved towards middle age and the children towards adulthood.

Chapter 4

The seasons treated the Gregory family kindly with not many droughts or floods; they had surely chosen wisely the place to put down roots and become part of this energetic young country.

They all took part in the social life of the district. Their friends varied from those born in the colony, new settlers from Great Britain, even those whose parents had been convicts and gone on to make a success of their lives.

The Gregorys bred rams to sell and it was at one of these sales that David met a young man from the northern tablelands who was looking to expand his flock. His name was Jack Harrison and he was tall and fair with bright blue eyes and a hearty laugh. His sense of humour was infectious and David was impressed. He asked him home to dinner the next night.

'Whereabouts exactly is your property?' asked Adam.

'On the northern tablelands, about seventy miles north-east of Armidale.'

'Armidale?' Milly piped up. 'I've never heard of it!'

'It's a pretty little town,' Jack continued. 'My family has lived in the district for about twenty years. My father died about a year ago, and my older brother has taken over the family property to the west of the township. I have bought a place to the east.'

'Do you have any other family?' Sophia asked kindly.

'Yes, my mother is still alive and I have two sisters,' Jack replied.

'Is it very cold there?' Caroline asked.

'Well, certainly a lot colder than here,' Jack laughed. 'The winters can be a bit grim. There are plenty of frosts and the occasional fall of snow. On the other hand, the summer is pleasant, doesn't get too hot, and it's a hot dry heat.'

'How wonderful,' Sophia commented. 'I'll never forget the first summer we spent here. I thought I'd never get used to it.'

'You should try the northern tablelands then. The climate is perfect for people like you, people who are used to cooler weather.'

'I don't think you'd be able to persuade my husband to leave here,' Caroline remarked. 'He loves it here and he loves the heat.'

'Well, you must come for a visit, and you can find out for yourselves. My house isn't finished yet but my mother really loves having visitors.'

A thrill shivered down Milly's spine every time Jack's blue eyes caught hers.

Jack was puzzled by Milly's connection with the others, so when David took him back to Maitland he asked, 'Milly is your cousin?'

'Yes.'

Jack thought she seemed so much part of the family but he could not help asking, 'So she's just on a visit?'

'No, her mother died when she was born and she has lived with us ever since.'

Not liking to ask what had happened to her father, Jack went on, 'She's a lovely girl.'

'Bit of a spitfire sometimes, but we all get on well,' David laughed, a little amused at his new friend's interest.

Jack returned to Maitland six months later and made sure to get in touch with the Gregory family.

'I think he's keen on you,' David teased Milly.

'Don't be silly.' Milly flushed with embarrassment.

'Why shouldn't he be?' Caroline remarked. 'Our Milly is a lovely young woman.'

This was too much for Milly so she retreated to the safety of her room.

Travelling to and from Armidale had been made easier by the construction of the railway from Sydney to Armidale and so, with the excuse of buying more stock for his property, Jack's visits became more frequent. He insisted that they come and visit him and his family. He was eager to show them the beauty of the tablelands.

'My mother and sisters would really love to meet you all and we could then visit my place. It's lovely up there in the autumn.'

It was decided that the whole family would be 'too much of a good thing', so it was only Sophia, Caroline and the two girls who returned with Jack after his next visit.

'You're sure it won't be too tiring for you?' Adam asked his mother.

'Of course not!' Sophia was indignant. 'Besides I would like to meet Jack's family.'

'He seems very fond of Milly,' Caroline remarked. 'As she does of him,' she added.

'He's a really nice man,' said Sophia, 'and I'm sure he would take great care of Milly.' Sophia's voice quavered a little as she added, 'it just seems such a long way away.'

'Well, you'll soon find out if he is a suitable person for Milly.'

Adam wondered how his mother would cope with Milly's absence. She had protected and cared for her from the moment she was born.

'It's going to be hard on mother,' Adam confided in Caroline. 'That is if Milly does go off and live in the back of beyond.'

Caroline giggled. 'I wouldn't exactly call Armidale the back of beyond.'

The visit would turn out to be a great success.

Jack's older brother Graham met them at the railway station and took them in their sulky to the family property. Jack arrived with his sisters and their husbands a little later. Sophia's fears were put to rest; they seemed a charming, friendly, easy-going family and she could see they would make Milly most welcome.

A day later, Jack and his mother accompanied Sophia, Caroline, Milly and Sophie to Glenfoyle, his property north-east of Armidale, a little east of the small village of Guyra.

Milly was impressed by the rolling hills and attractive views to the north. 'This is lovely country,' she enthused, 'isn't it Grandma?'

'Yes it is,' but Sophia's heart sank a little, the enigmatic gum trees always made her long for England's trees.

Jack had only just finished building his house with the help of a local builder, so it was all fresh and new. There was basic furniture, enough beds, enough chairs, a kitchen table, a dining table, but it obviously needed a woman's touch. There was no garden, actually no fence to keep the sheep, horses and cows from coming too close to the house.

'That's the next thing on the list,' he announced cheerfully. 'We're going to build a fence so that I can have a garden, grow vegetables and fruit trees, that sort of thing.'

He glanced at Milly to see her reaction to his home, which he hoped would be here home as well in the not too distant future. 'I think it's lovely,' she said excitedly. She could imagine living there with Jack. It would be perfect.

When Jack took them to the other side of the hills that surrounded his house, Milly exclaimed. 'It's beautiful!' she announced excitedly as she saw row up row of hills that stretched into the distance. 'How far north does your land go?' she asked.

'About six miles, beyond the third or fourth row of hills it drops two thousand feet into gulf country, and that's the boundary of my land.'

It seemed the land he owned stretched almost to forever.

'Gulf country? What's it like?'

'Very steep, rough, and unfortunately where the dingoes breed.'

'Are they a problem?' Sophia enquired.

'Well yes, they kill and maim a lot of sheep and lambs. We have to bring back the ewes closer to this end when they are lambing.'

But nothing could dim Milly's joy in being with Jack and seeing where he lived. Would she live here one day? Yes, yes, yes please, she thought to herself.

Jack came down to the Hunter in the spring and formally asked Sophia for Milly's hand in marriage. They had been writing frequent letters to each other and Sophia knew his proposal was inevitable.

'I love her very much, and will do my best to look after her and make her happy.'

'I think you are a fine young man,' Sophia answered, 'but I'm just a little worried Milly might be lonely, so far away from us all.'

'But you can come and visit as often as you wish, and I'll make sure she isn't lonely.'

'Then you have my blessing,' Sophia consented.

Milly and Jack were married the following summer. Sophia felt a quiver of anxiety as she bade the young couple goodbye; a shadow seemed to momentarily darken her spirits. She shrugged it off, 'I'm just sad because she's going so far away' she told herself. Looking into the eyes of the young couple who were glowing with excitement and happiness, she chided herself. What could go wrong when there was so much love in their hearts?

When Milly and Jack arrived at Glenfoyle, Milly felt that all her dreams had come true. Jack was her husband, this was her home, and she would be happy forever and ever. At last she was no longer the outsider, the one who did not quite fit. Although the Gregory family loved and cared for her, there was that little look of pity, a desire to be especially kind to the motherless and fatherless child.

Milly laughed. Now she could be truly herself free of the past and the vain regrets. Jack would make sure of that. As far as dreams go Milly would make sure this one had a happy ending. But why think about endings? Her dream was just beginning.

•

'Come on Demelza, are you going to help us in the garden or not?' John demanded.

'Of course I am.' she replied tartly. 'And I wish you'd call me Mel.'

'Because only me and the dreaded Miss Logan call you Demelza,' John laughed.

'Stop teasing your sister.' Milly interjected. 'It's a shame, Demelza is such a pretty name.'

She had bowed to her daughter's wishes about her name when her daughter had told her how nasty the same Miss Logan had been when Demelza was at school in Armidale. The brother and sister had gone to Rock Abbey school when they were a good deal younger. At first Jack had taken them to school in the buggie and Milly had brought them home but when it was considered safe for them to do so, they rode their horses. And then Demelza had stayed with her Aunt Margaret, Jack's sister, in Armidale for her final year at school, and there had incurred Miss Logan's dislike for some reason.

Johnny had refused to leave home and finish his education in Armidale. 'I'll learn more staying at home and letting my father teach me how to run a property,' he explained.

Johnny had born eighteen months after Jack and Milly were married. He was named after both Jack's father and Milly's grandfather, but had been called Johnny from the start. He was very like his father in looks, but lacked his father's easy going jovial nature. Sometimes Milly had difficulty understanding her quiet and introverted son, but loved him none the less.

When Demelza was born a year later Jack couldn't disguise the look of surprise on his face when he saw his little red-haired, green-eyed daughter.

Milly laughed at him. 'My mother had red hair,' she explained. 'Of course I never saw her, but that's what Grandma told me,' she added, a little sadly.

When Adam and Caroline saw the baby girl, they could not believe their eyes.

'She's just like Amelia.' Adam felt quite emotional at the thought of his dead sister. 'I'm glad mother's not here. I think it would have upset her terribly.'

Sophia had died suddenly but peacefully soon after Johnny was born. She died content in the knowledge that Adam and his family and Milly and her family were happy and prosperous.

Caroline did not agree with her husband. 'I think your mother would have been thrilled that there was another little girl who looked just like her daughter.'

As she grew older, the likeness between Demelza and her grandmother Amelia became more and more apparent. Every time Adam and Caroline saw her their hearts would stop for a minute.

'You know, Milly,' Adam explained, 'Demelza is just like your mother.'

Milly turned away. Why do they keep reminding me? she thought. I never saw my mother, I wish they'd stop talking about it.

'So you always say.' She sounded impatient.

Oh, oh, thought Adam, I've put my foot in it. I'd better stop talking about Amelia. What a shame, she was such a lovely girl and I just wanted Milly to know that. Adam changed his tactics. 'And you Milly, you look more like your grandmother every day.'

'Do I?' Milly flushed with pleasure. 'But I do miss her. I miss her so much.'

'We all do.' Adam agreed.

Demelza made sure she didn't sleep in the next morning. She had the fires lit and the porridge cooking before anyone else appeared.

'Well, we are the early bird this morning!' Johnny teased.

Demelza ignored him.

'What are you boys doing today?' Milly enquired.

'I think we'll check on the sheep in the bottom paddocks and make sure the roos haven't broken any fences,' Johnny told her.

Demelza giggled. 'Are all the jelly beans going with you?'

'Hush, child,' Milly reprimanded. 'You shouldn't call them jelly beans.'

There were noises on the back verandah, the sounds of boots clumping on the wooden floor and of voices, men talking.

'Well, there they are,' Demelza went on.

'I hope they didn't hear you call them jelly beans.'

'Of course they didn't,' Demelza laughed, 'anyway they wouldn't mind, it suits them perfectly.'

The young men's real names were Gary, Barry and Larry and they were the sons of the first worker Jack had employed, Fingal Kelly. His wife, who had bestowed her favours rather generously before he had married her, already had two sons but the last of the boys was his. Barry was tall, thin and dark, Gary was fair and stocky, and Larry looked like his father. Hence the nickname, the jelly beans, as they were all different sizes and colours. Their father had been unable to continue working after hurting his back, so now the boys worked for Jack. They were honest, tried hard, but were a little slow and needed constant supervision and constant reminders on how to do their work. Nevertheless, they were good natured and inoffensive so Jack and Johnny, although sometimes frustrated by their ineptitude, took it all with good humour.

The trio of brothers also had a sister, Polly, who helped Milly and Demelza on wash day, scrubbed floors, swept and cleaned windows. She was a very quiet girl but she did her best and Milly didn't complain about her lack of conversation. Demelza would try and get her to talk, but was met with a stony silence most of the time. So the boys were called the jelly beans and their sister, whose full name was Pelemenza, was nicknamed Jolly Polly, as anyone less jolly than Polly would be hard to find.

Although they lived in the so-called 'back of beyond', this did not stop the Harrisons from enjoying a lively social life. Jack's sisters Margaret and Jean lived in Armidale and because Demelza had lived with both aunts when she attended school in Armidale, she knew her aunts, uncles and cousins well. As it took two days to reach Armidale from Glenfoyle, any of the family making the trip broke the journey with other cousins at Rockvale. Jack's mother, older brother and his family lived near Guyra, thirty miles west of Glenfoyle and twenty-five miles north of Armidale. The families always gathered for birthdays, Easter and Christmas, and of course Milly went to Maitland at least once a year to visit her family, and they often visited in return. Such invitations were not for lunch or dinner, but for the weekend and when visiting Maitland, stretched to a week or even two.

Demelza loved her little part of the world, but had no understanding of how different their lives were from those of her mother and grandmother, who had been members of the English aristocracy with all its advantages and limitations. Her Great-uncle Adam was the only one who could remember this long-lost life but he rarely spoke of it and much preferred his life in Australia. As a family, they had completely lost touch with his great-uncle William, did not even know if his family still lived at Melrose

Park and didn't care. The striking likeness of Demelza to Amelia was the only thing that gave Adam a sense of loss, but it was for the loss of a sister, not of his country. He knew it upset Milly if he talked about her mother so he refrained from doing so.

When Milly and Demelza planned to offer hospitality in return to the Harrison relations for weekends or the Gregory relations for a week or more, they went into a flurry of cleaning the house, making beds, baking cakes and biscuits, making sure Jack had killed enough meat and picked enough vegetables and fruit. Jack milked two cows every morning so there was always plenty of milk and cream. They usually only had visitors in late spring, summer and early autumn. Although there were open fires in the kitchen and the little-used lounge room, the bedrooms were freezing in winter and guests would have needed a lot more blankets and eiderdowns to combat the frosty nights. Although Glenfoyle was 1000 feet higher than Armidale, the climate was a little milder. Wisely Jack had planted pine trees to the south and west of his house to keep out the icy south-west winds that seemed to blow directly from the South Pole. Summers, fortunately, were cool which pleased Milly and especially Demelza with her red hair and fair skin inherited directly from her Scottish ancestors.

The property to the west of Glenfoyle had been on the market for some time as the previous owner had died and his widow had returned to live with her family in Sydney. Then, one day, word came that it had been sold. Demelza and Johnny were curious to hear about their new neighbours.

'Their name is McDougall and they have one son,' Jack explained. 'I believe they had a small place near Sydney but when their father died he apparently left his son enough money to buy a larger property.'

'I wonder why they wanted to come up here when they were used to living in Sydney,' Demelza speculated.

'They probably know nothing about running a property,' Johnny said scornfully. 'Then we'll have to help them.' As usual Jack was friendly and concerned.

'Poor things,' Milly volunteered. 'They won't know anyone – unless they have relations here.'

'I don't think they have any,' Jack responded.

'Then we must have them all to lunch. Do you know how old their son is?'

Jack shook his head. 'No idea.'

'The dead father was probably a convict,' Johnny was determined not to like them. Demelza giggled. 'Don't be silly, Johnny, not everyone in Australia is descended from a convict. Besides how could he have made a lot of money if he was a convict?'

'Don't know, but mark my words, you'll find there's something, something...'

'Don't talk nonsense Johnny,' Jack reproved his son. 'They're our new neighbours and we'll do our best to be friendly and helpful, wherever they have come from, won't we, Milly?'

'There is no harm in being kind to people less fortunate than you are,' Milly pointed out

'Less fortunate? I thought they had a lot of money,' Johnny insisted.

'It doesn't look like it,' Jack said drily.

'Perhaps they're escaping from the law,' Johnny said.

'Oh Johnny you do talk a lot of rubbish,' Demelza was getting impatient with her brothers attitude.

'Mark my words, no good will come of it,' Johnny predicted.

'Come of what?' Demelza asked.

Milly intervened. 'We'll have them all to lunch say, the weekend after next. Johnny, you can go and visit them and extend the invitation.'

'Thanks a lot.' He stumped out of the room.

Jack sighed. 'Sometimes I don't know what's wrong with that boy.'

'He's just naturally grumpy,' Demelza tried to explain, 'but he didn't get that from either of you.'

Milly sighed. Perhaps he was like her long-lost father whom she had never known.

And then the subject was dropped.

After the ice was broken and the lunch took place, the McDougall son, Alec, started calling on the Harrisons, asking Jack's advice about the problems they were having, and Jack was only too happy to try to help the boy who so obviously knew little about sheep, dingoes or anything to do with running a property.

'I wonder where they really did come from?' Jack pondered.

'As if they'd tell us,' Johnny sneered. 'But I know why he keeps calling in, to see Demelza of course.'

His sister went pink. 'Don't be silly.'

Johnny started teasing her about his visits. 'Demelza, your boyfriend's coming.'

Sometimes she would be so annoyed with her brother that she shut herself in her bedroom until poor Alec had departed. He was always polite and respectful and much more interesting than other young men she had met. He was also tall and good-looking, and when he smiled Demelza felt her heart race. She kept her feelings to herself. Perhaps it was because they knew so little about the family that she found him intriguing.

One morning Jack and Johnny had gone down the paddock to help a cow who was having trouble calving. They could be away for an hour or all day depending on the circumstances. Demelza was ironing and Milly had just made some biscuits when Alec arrived, white-faced looking worried.

'What's the matter, Alec?' Milly asked kindly.

'It's my mother. She's had a bad turn, and my father has gone to fix the flood gates. I'm supposed to go and help him as soon as I can but I don't want to leave her alone.'

Milly was concerned for Mrs McDougall. 'You'd like me to come and sit with her until you can both get home?'

'I was just getting ready to leave when I heard a crash. She had fainted on the kitchen floor. I managed to get her onto her bed and I gave her a cup of tea. She seems a little better now but I don't like leaving her alone.'

'Of course I'll come and sit with her. I think there's a horse in the yard. You go on with the ironing, Mel and I'll go with Alec and see how his mother is.'

Alec and Demelza waited at the gate while Milly saddled the horse. Alone at last, but Demelza didn't know what to say. She looked at Alec.

'Is Alec short for anything?' Demelza finally asked.

'Well yes, my name is Alexander. I was named after my grandfather and apparently my mother did not like him so she always called me Alec.'

More and more mysterious, Demelza thought. I'd love to find out more about the McDougall family.

'Oh well, Alec's a nice name anyway,' she sympathised.

'I think Demelza's a lovely name,' Alec replied.

She flushed, didn't know what to say next, looked at Alec and thought he wants to tell me something. I wonder what it is?

Then Milly came back on the horse she had saddled. 'You'll be alright?' she asked Demelza.

'Of course, I'll finish the ironing. Father and Johnny should be back soon, anyway.'

Alec turned to say goodbye to Demelza. His look was one of despair, entreaty, longing.

'I wonder what he wanted to say,' she thought.

It wasn't what he wanted to say but what he wanted to do. He longed to take her in his arms, kiss the sweetly soft lips, bury his head in her glorious red hair.

He and Milly rode off to the McDougall's home.

For the rest of his life Alec regretted that he had not done any of these, regretted he had not declared his honourable intentions, regretted he had not told her he worshipped the ground on which she walked and regretted he had not told her that she was the most beautiful girl in the world. If he had said or done even one of those things, life could have been so different.

The next time Alec called, Jack and Johnny were preparing to go down to the paddock to check the sheep for worms and blowfly strike. Jack suggested Alec come with them.

'Yes, that would be very helpful. I'd like to see what you do,' Alec agreed.

'Your father is not expecting you to help him?' Jack asked.

'No, he's actually doing some bookwork today.' Alex replied.

Johnny rolled his eyes upwards as if to intimate he was surprised that Hamish McDougall could do bookwork. Probably can't read and write, he thought to himself.

Jack, seeing Alec's despairing looks at Demelza felt sorry for the lad. 'How about you coming too, Demelza? A bit of fresh air will do you good.'

'What a good idea, I'll just go and ask mother, we were going to do some cooking.'

She reappeared a few minutes later wearing her riding clothes and with a large hat firmly attached to her head.

They rode around the hill that blocked the view of the row upon and row of hills that stretched to the horizon. When they were first married, Milly had asked Jack why he hadn't built his house to take advantage of the beautiful view.

'You have to build a house close to a good water supply,' he'd explained. 'You can't always rely on rain water and there is a spring that never dries up even in the longest drought. Also the hills to the north and west protect us from those freezing western winds.'

Milly thought this was all very practical but she would have built the house to take advantage of the view.

As the four rode round the hill, Demelza stopped and gazed to the north. 'Isn't it beautiful?' she said. 'This must be the most beautiful place in the world.'

'Yes, it's very lovely,' Alec agreed, but he didn't mean the view.

They ambled down the paddock enjoying the sunshine. The sheep they were looking for were in the next paddock. Jack explained to Alec some of the finer points or rearing sheep. Johnny was in a mood and wouldn't join in. Demelza trotted to the edge of a slope and turned. 'This is where I'd build a house.'

She looked at Alec and smiled, a most beautiful smile that would haunt him for the rest of his life. Then they made their way to the gate into the next paddock. Demelza was a little way ahead of her companions when her horse seemed to stumble, then it reared throwing Demelza to the ground. In horror, Jack, Johnny and Alec saw the black snake had spooked Demelza's horse slithering away. She lay very still. Jack and Johnny leapt from the saddle and dashed to her side as Alec followed, a terrible feeling of apprehension tearing through him.

Jack knelt down. 'Mel, Mel, are you okay?' She did not move. He felt for the pulse in her throat. Nothing. 'Mel, Mel,' he cried, mounting desperation in his voice.

He knelt closer; the girl was lying still, so very still. 'She's not breathing.' He looked at Johnny and Alec his voice breaking with fear. 'Mel, talk to us,' Johnny was crying.

Alec looked on numb with horror. This couldn't be happening, not to Demelza. Not to his darling Demelza.

'Give her a minute, she'll come round.' Johnny couldn't believe the horrible reality.

'She's not breathing,' Jack said quietly.

'She will in a minute, you'll see,' Johnny sobbed.

Jack shook his head.

'What can we do?' Alec asked.

Jack and Johnny were both silent.

'There must be something,' Alec implored.

'It's all your fault,' Johnny yelled.

'The horse was spooked by a snake. It was an accident.' Jack was icily calm. 'If I get on my horse, you give Demelza to me, Johnny. I'll hold her and you can lead my horse.'

Slowly and silently they made their way home. When they reached the horse yard Jack lowered Demelza to Johnny, got down and then cradled his daughter in his arms.

'Is there anything I can do?' asked a devastated Alec.

'Yes, put the saddles in the shed and let the horses go,' Jack managed to mutter.

Carrying the lifeless body of his daughter, Jack walked with Johnny to the house. Milly saw them coming and ran to meet them. 'What's wrong? What's happened? Is she hurt?'

'Hurt?' Johnny screamed. 'She's dead and it's all that fellow's fault, it's all Alec's fault.' 'She can't be, she can't be,' Milly whispered, but the look on Jack's face told her it was so.

Jack laid Demelza gently on her bed. Milly knelt beside her, stroking her hand. 'My lovely little girl, my beautiful girl.' Johnny stood sobbing. Jack knelt beside his wife and put his arms round her shaking body. He looked over her shoulder. 'Johnny, go and make your mother a cup of tea, and put some whisky in it. Bring me a whisky.'

They knelt together for some time. Milly looked at Jack. Her eyes were glazed with horror. 'My dear wife, you must be very brave,' Jack whispered.

Milly started to tremble uncontrollably. Johnny arrived with the tea and whisky.

'My dear, you must drink all your tea,' Jack ordered gently but insistently.

She did as she was told and the trembling eased a little. 'Let's go into the kitchen where it's warm,' Jack suggested.

'No, no I won't leave her. Don't you see I can't leave her alone.' Tears streamed down her cheeks.

Jack took Johnny away from where was Milly grieving over Demelza's motionless body. 'This is what I want you to do,' he explained to his son. 'As early as you can in the morning get the sulky ready for me to take Milly and Demelza into Guyra to my brother's. When you have helped us load up, I'd like you to take your horse and ride ahead of us as fast as you can and tell my brother what has happened, and to expect us a few hours later. Tonight I will give you a letter to take down to the Kellys and ask Barry to ride to Armidale and deliver it to my sister, Margaret. I'll ask them to come to Guyra as soon as they can, but in the meantime send a letter to the Gregorys in Maitland asking them to come to Armidale. We'll delay the funeral until they can get here. Now do you understand all that?'

'Yes, father, I'll do my very best,' Johnny complied.

'And another thing. I don't want you repeating that you think it was Alec McDougall's fault. A snake spooked Demelza's horse, I saw it. Do I have your promise in this?'

'Yes, father.'

The next morning they all set off in accordance with Jack's plans. Wrapping Demelza in a bedspread he gently laid her in the sulky. Before leaving, Jack insisted Milly have some breakfast then the grieving parents set off with Johnny galloping ahead.

Milly sat and shivered, barely noticing what was happening. Her eyes were blank with grief. It was a fine sunny day but she felt cold, her body was cold, her soul was cold. Jack spoke to her, gentle comforting words, but she couldn't hear what he said.

It seemed such a long trip. Jack was worried Milly would collapse. But somehow she managed to sit beside him, shivering but upright.

At last they arrived in Guyra. Jack's family surrounded Milly, Jack and Johnny with love and comfort, but how could anyone bear such a terrible event?

Later the next day Jack's sisters, Margaret and Barbara, along with their families arrived from Armidale. Milly did not seem to know what was happening, but dutifully did everything Jack suggested. Jack made the funeral arrangements and they planned to stay in Armidale to await the arrival of Milly's relations.

'Milly dear,' Jack suggested, 'if you don't feel well enough Margaret or Sophie will stay with you.'

She shook her head. 'I must go. I must say goodbye to my little girl.' The tears streamed down her cheeks.

After the funeral, Sophie suggested that Milly come back to Maitland with them. 'Of course you and Johnny are also welcome,' she added.

'Thank you Sophie,' Jack replied, 'but Johnny and I will have to check on things at Glenfoyle. I think it would be a good idea if Milly returns with you, and please take her to a doctor. The local doctor has prescribed some sleeping pills for her but I think she will need some more.' He shook his head. 'She is so devastated, I worry for her.' Jack's voice broke; he had been keeping an icy control on his own emotions, but it had been a taxing effort.

Before they left, Milly said to Jack, 'Please don't touch any of Demelza's things,' she was adamant. 'I want her room left just as it is.'

'Of course, my dear,' he promised.

A silent Jack and Johnny returned to Glenfoyle. The house was eerily quiet. It was unbearable. 'We must keep busy,' Jack told his desperately upset son. 'Work, that's the best thing to do.'

That night Jack heard Johnny sobbing and at last he let his own feelings come to the surface and lay in his bed, weeping for his beautiful daughter and his traumatised wife.

•

After a month Milly decided it was time to return home. 'I have to get back to look after Jack and Johnny,' she explained to Sophie.

'Of course, but are you sure you feel well enough?' Sophie asked.

Milly shrugged. 'I have to face it some time. You have all been so kind, Sophie. I do thank you.'

Sophie's heart twisted as she looked into Milly's haunted face. 'I'll come with you, and I'll see about train bookings and tell the rest of the family.'

'Thank you Sophie, you've been so good to me,' Milly said.

Jack and Johnny met them in Armidale, and Milly felt encouraged by their expression of love and comfort. Everyone knew how hard it was going to be for Milly to come back to Glenfoyle – a Glenfoyle without Demelza. Sophie and James stayed for a few days.

'Would you like us to help you tidy up Demelza's room?' Sophie asked hesitantly.

'No, thank you. I don't want any of her things touched,' Milly replied sharply.

'Of course Milly, I understand.' But did she? How could anyone understand, Milly wondered.

Milly did her best during the weeks that followed. She cleaned, washed, ironed, gardened, cooked, all the things she had always done but the pain in her heart was unbearable. Through it all, she still managed to notice there was no sign of the neighbours.

'Where are the McDougalls?' she asked Jack.

'Hamish left a letter for me which I found under the kitchen door,' Jack explained. 'Apparently his wife had taken a bad turn and they had taken her in to hospital in Armidale. He decided that when Agnes recovered they would make their way to Queensland, so they are selling their place next door, and as far as I know they have already gone to Queensland.'

Milly was surprised but glad that she didn't have to face Agnes after the things Johnny had said about Demelza's accident. Johnny was glad they had left; he thought there was something funny about the whole family and he couldn't stand Alec.

The months went by and there did not seem to be any improvement in Milly's condition. Jack came up with an idea. Milly had inherited the block next to the Gregorys on her twenty-first birthday, but she had never taken any interest in it. One day Jack asked her if she would like to move to Maitland where they could build a new house on Milly's block and she would be close to her relations.

'You mean you and Johnny would come too?'

'Of course, you know I would do anything for you,' Jack insisted.

'No, no, no, you and Johnny love it here. I couldn't ask you to do that, but thank you for the offer.'

Jack put his arm round his wife's shoulders. 'I love you, Milly, I would do anything for you.' She shook her head but her eyes filled with tears. 'Are you sure, Milly?'

'Quite sure. I don't want to leave Glenfoyle. I don't want to leave Demelza,' she added quietly. Jack understood; he didn't bring the subject up again.

•

A distraught white-faced Alec arrived home the day of Demelza's accident. He slumped in a chair and covered his face with his hands.

'What's the matter, Alec?' his mother enquired.

Alec groaned. Something was terribly wrong.

His father looked at his wife, then his son. 'What is wrong?'

Alec groaned again then his shoulders started shaking. 'It's Demelza,' he croaked. 'She's dead.'

Hamish and Agnes looked at each other in astonishment. 'Dead? What do you mean?'

Finally Alec managed to tell the sad story. 'We were riding down the paddock, and a snake spooked her horse. She fell and hit her head, and she died.'

'That's terrible, my boy.' His father was concerned by his son's behaviour.

'I loved her, she was so beautiful, so sweet, and I loved her.'

'My poor boy.' Agnes put her arms around her son. Hamish didn't know what to do or say.

'And what's worse, Johnny was so upset he told lies when we brought her home. He told his mother it was my fault!'

This time it was Hamish who groaned. 'I'm sure it wasn't your fault.'

'It wasn't, it wasn't. I was nowhere near her when the horse shied,' Alex insisted.

'I'm so sorry, Alec.' His mother tried to be comforting. 'I know you were very fond of Demelza. I'll make you a nice cup of tea.'

'What good is a cup of tea when Demelza's dead?' Agnes and Hamish didn't know what to do or say.

'I'm sorry, Alec,' his father muttered 'But try and pull yourself together, you're upsetting your mother and she isn't very well.'

Alec drank the tea and tried to control himself.

'I'm very sorry the girl died, but did Johnny really say it was your fault?'

'Yes he did. He's never liked me and I suppose he'll tell everyone it was my fault.'

'Did Jack see the snake?'

'Yes, but the whole district is going to think I did it.'

Hamish was silent for a long time.

'This is serious,' he said to his wife later. 'If Johnny tells everyone this story they will start asking questions about who we are and where we come from.' He was silent again. Then, 'We came here because we thought we'd escape from the gossip about my father being a convict.'

'But you have always said he was innocent, that he didn't do the thing he was transported to Australia for,' Agnes reminded him.

'Yes, yes, I know he was innocent. He never touched the girl he was accused of attacking, but if they start saying Alec killed Demelza, it will all come out and our lives made miserable. We thought we were going to get away from all that.'

'I know, I know, you did your best to find a way for us to have a better life.'

'My father served ten years for something he didn't do. I'm not having my son go through the same thing,' Hamish said bitterly. 'We must leave.'

'Leave? When... how can we?'

'Tomorrow.'

Agnes started to feel faint. 'Hamish, I feel a bit giddy I think I'll go and lie down.'

'Of course, don't worry I'll work everything out and we'll be gone before the Harrisons come.'

He went to Alec who was sitting quietly, his face drawn with grief and pain.

'We must leave here,' Hamish told him, 'before the Harrisons start poking their noses into our affairs. I want you to pack all your clothes and we'll see what your mother would like to take. I hope we'll be ready to go in the morning.'

Hamish and Alec spent most of the night packing. Agnes slept fitfully moaning in her sleep from time to time. When she awoke, Hamish instructed her to pack all her clothes and a few kitchen items like cups, plates and cutlery.

'What about the furniture?' Agnes asked.

'We'll leave all that. It's only rubbish anyway,' Hamish added bitterly. He turned to Alec. 'I'd like you to go to the Kellys and ask them if they would feed the dogs and chooks because we have to take your mother into Armidale as she is very ill. We don't know when we will be back.'

'What about the horses?' Alec asked.

'We'll need one of them for the sulky, then you and I can take turns riding and leading the other two. Bring all their gear, the saddles and stuff. It's going to be a long day. We may not get to Armidale before dark so we'll be needing blankets and pillows.'

Alec felt numb. How could things have gone so terribly wrong in the space of a day?

Luckily the next day was warm and sunny. Hamish asked Agnes to choose any small things she was particularly fond of and they were packed in amongst the clothes.

'You mean we're not coming back?' Agnes asked in surprise.

'No, we're not coming back. We'll sell this place and move to Queensland where it's warmer.' He shivered but not with the cold. 'First of all we must get you better. We'll see a doctor as soon as we get to Armidale.'

It was a slow laborious trip. Hamish didn't wish to go too fast in case the jolting upset Agnes. On the other hand she looked so ill he wondered if they would get her to see a doctor in time. Agnes slept in the sulky about ten miles from Armidale, made as comfortable as her husband could with blankets and pillows. Hamish and Alec slept on the ground.

As soon as the sun came up they were on their way again. Hamish took Agnes straight to the hospital. She had trouble breathing and was a very bad colour.

'Don't worry Mr McDougall, we'll look after her,' the sister said comfortingly.

'Now I've some business to do,' Hamish told Alec. 'Stay with your mother.'

'Of course, father,' the boy replied.

Hamish went straight to the stock and station agent Neill Mitchell, told him he wanted to sell 'Brookdale' as soon as possible, that his wife was ill and they were moving to Queensland as soon as his wife was better.

'And if there are any enquiries, I would prefer it if you suggested we had already left for Queensland.'

Neill was an obliging man – as most stock and station agents are – and didn't think there was anything unusual in Hamish's request.

A little way out of Armidale, Hamish found a boarding house where he and Alec could stay, with space in the boarding house yard for their sulky and horses.

On returning to the hospital and finding there was no change in Agnes's condition, he and Alec went to the boarding house to get some sleep.

'You don't think the trouble over Demelza made my mother ill?' Alec asked.

'No, not entirely, she hasn't been very well for some time,' his father assured him. 'High blood pressure the doctor in Sydney told me.'

'She certainly doesn't look very well.'

'No lad, she doesn't. I'm afraid, I'm very much afraid we might lose her.'

Alec bit his lip. He must keep his emotions under control somehow.

At the hospital next morning they were met by a solemn-faced sister. 'I'm afraid your wife had a massive stroke in the night Mr McDougall. She can neither move nor speak.'

'Is she going to die?' Alec blurted out.

'We don't know. It is possible.'

They went to the room where Agnes lay so still and unresponsive, her eyes open but unseeing.

'I've… I've got to go outside for a minute,' Alec choked and staggered from the room.

Then it was just a matter of waiting, waiting for Agnes to recover or die, waiting to sell their property. Hamish and Alec took turns sitting with her. They talked to her, tried to get some response but there was none.

•

Ironically, Adam Gregory inherited Melrose Park, the estate in England where he had grown up and which had belonged first to his grandfather, then to his nasty Uncle William who had told his father John he must leave. Adam's cousin William had become a dissolute wastrel after his parents died and he spent most of the money on gambling and loose living in the East Indies. Because he was homosexual there was no hope of an heir. When he died from liver damage caused by alcohol poisoning Adam inherited the family estate.

Adam was shocked and surprised when he received a letter from his cousin's lawyer asking for his instructions. Caroline wondered why her husband burst into shouts of laughter.

'It's ours,' he said. 'It's ours, can you believe it?'

He had no intention of returning to England, he and all his family were happily settled in Australia. He wrote to the lawyer instructing him to sell Melrose Park for the best price he could.

Then he wrote to Jack, suggesting that with his new-found wealth he could buy Milly's block and that Milly and Jack and Johnny would thereby receive a considerable sum of money. He asked Jack to be very tactful with Milly; he didn't want to hurt her feelings but he knew Milly. She had never taken any interest in the land she had inherited from her father.

Jack, Milly and Johnny discussed the situation, and Jack suggested hesitantly that they could buy the property next door, 'Brookdale', which the McDougalls had previously owned.

'What a great idea,' enthused Johnny. 'We could put another man on, and you could spend more time with mother. Why you could even have a holiday.'

'Would you like that, Milly? We could go to Maitland, or Sydney or the coast. Which would you like best?'

'The place may have been sold already,' Milly said flatly.

'Well, I'll go into Armidale tomorrow, and if it hasn't been sold I'll put a deposit on it until the money comes through from Adam.'

Johnny was disappointed with his mother's lack of interest.

Later that night after Milly had gone to bed, he asked his father why his mother was still so upset. 'She has you and me,' Johnny's feelings were hurt. 'I just don't think she cares about me at all.'

'Of course she does, she loves you, it's just that - well, she's still suffering from shock. We just have to give her time and she'll be her old self again.'

'I don't think so,' Johnny said gloomily, 'I think when Demelza died my mother died too.' He stomped off to bed wondering if life would ever be worth living again.

The next day, Jack took aside Milly and asked her to tell him why she couldn't believe in his and Johnny's love and that he would do anything to help her.

'Don't you see, it's all my fault...' Milly started to say.

Jack hushed her, made a cup of tea and calmed her with soft words and hugs and gently took her to their room, undressed her and put her to bed.

'I don't deserve you. You are so good to me.' Milly said.

'Hush now, Milly, try and get some sleep, things will get better you'll see.'

He had slipped a sleeping pill into her tea so he knew she would sleep.

All the arrangements for the purchase of 'Brookdale' were made. Adam paid the balance owing when the money from Adam came through. He asked the estate agent if he knew where the McDougalls had gone. Neill Mitchell shook his head. 'The old man said he thought they'd make their way to Queensland, I have to transfer the money to a bank in Tenterfield, but I don't really know.'

•

Milly never recovered from Demelza's death. She went about her household tasks like a little lost soul. She didn't eat very much in spite of Jack's encouragement and grew more and more frail.

On a spring morning in 1912 Jack got up as usual to light the fires and make the cup of tea that he usually took to his wife. She hadn't moved since he had got out of bed and when he said her name she didn't stir.

Putting the tea down on the bedside table he leant over her. 'Milly, I've brought your tea.'

There was no reply. He touched her forehead. It was cold, very cold. Then he realised she wasn't breathing and that her lips were blue.

'Milly! Milly!' he called in despair, but Milly had gone. Her torment was over. Her dream of a happy life with Jack, Johnny and Demelza disappeared into the mists of time.

Would there be a red-haired, green-eyed girl in the future who could change their destiny?

Chapter 5

The two men stood on the platform of the Armidale railway station. They shook hands. Hamish boarded the train to make his way back to his old life. Alex mounted his horse and faced north on the way to his new life. He remembered his father's words when he desperately pleaded to let him go with him to Sydney.

'If you go back to Sydney, you'll always be a convict's grandson,' his father insisted. It will ruin your life. If you go north with a new name and enough money to set you up for the future you can do anything you want to.'

As Alec rode out of Armidale he did not know if he had the strength to face the future alone. Without his parents and with his dreams of a life with Demelza shattered. He arrived in Guyra, weary and aching. A few days later he had passed through Glen Innes and Deepwater. He knew he must reach Tenterfield where his father had promised to send him a letter at the post office.

'I get to Tenterfield,' he thought, 'then God knows what I'll do.'

He wandered around Tenterfield. It seemed a nice little town. 'Perhaps I can stay here for a while, nobody will know me. I could maybe get a job.'

He wandered into a stock and station agent's office. There was a tubby little man leafing through a newspaper and there was a tubby little girl by his side. He looked up, 'Can I help you?'

'Well, I wondered if there was, that is, I was hoping to get a job.'

The man looked at him with interest. 'What sort of job? Do you want to stay or are you just passing through?'

'It all depends,' was the reply.

'Depends on what?'

Alex felt embarrassed. He flushed. 'Well, if I can get a good job I'll stay a while.'

'What can you do?'

'Well I'm used to country life, I can ride and fence, that sort of thing.'

'Hmm, well, I have a small place just out of town, and sometimes I need someone here in the office, taking messages, that sort of thing. How does that interest you?'

'Yes,' Alex tried not to sound too eager.

'Consider yourself hired then, by the way what's your name?'

'It's......' there was a pause. 'It's Alex, Alex Douglas,' he said firmly.

'Well, I'm Michael Edwards, Mick for short, and this is my daughter Joan.'

'How do you do, sir,' Alex extended his hand and was surprised by Mick's strong grip. 'How do you do, Miss Edwards.'

Joan flushed with pleasure.

'Joan's mother died three years ago, so she looks after me.'

Alex nodded. 'Yes, I know what that's like, my parents died in an accident a while ago.'

Mick hoped he was not making a dreadful mistake hiring someone he knew nothing about. The boy was well-spoken and he looked gaunt and haggard; he had obviously seen bad times.

'You look as if you could do with a square meal. We'll find you somewhere to live, then you must come around and have dinner with us.'

They found him a room in a boarding house nearby. It was a poky and shabby little room, but Alex was grateful to have somewhere to lay his head, somewhere he could sleep and not worry what was going to happen the next day. Mick's cheerful optimism cut through the guilt and darkness that enveloped Alex, and little Joanie with her innocent childishness made Alex feel he was not doomed after all.

Slowly the crushing burden that had tormented Alex since the death of Demelza began to lift. He went about his duties, grateful to have something to do, eager to please Mick Edwards and make sure he kept his job.

After a while Mick suggested that Alex come and live with them. 'We have plenty of room,' he said, 'and seeing your wage isn't very high it means I don't feel guilty about paying you so little when you do so much for me.'

Joanie loved cooking and washing for Alex and followed him around like a little puppy dog, waiting for the crumbs of thanks that came from his lips. Even though Joanie was as yet only eleven, Alex shrewdly calculated to himself that in six or seven years he would marry her, and then his future would really be secure.

Mick kept a fatherly eye on Alex. Alex did not drink, worked hard and treated Joanie with respect. Mick was equally assured that Alex didn't act in any inappropriate ways with his daughter and could not fault him in that regard.

•

The years of the Great War in Europe were lean, nobody was buying or selling property, but Mick made a little money from his sheep and cattle. Alex eked out his meagre income by occasionally using some of his father's money but never so much that it would arouse suspicion. Alex played a waiting game, he just had to wait for Joanie to be old enough to marry, then his future would be secure. Occasionally he had dreams of a beautiful girl with long red hair and green eyes, and would be silent and moody for days, until the dreams faded.

Mick worried that Alex didn't seem to have any family or friends. He received no letters, no messages. At times he wondered if Alex was hiding from something dark that happened in his past, but the young man never spoke of his life before he came to Tenterfield. Alex had a fright one day when a man coming into the office looked at Alex with interest.

'I think I've met you before,' he said. 'Do you come from Armidale?'

'No,' Alex said curtly. 'Never been there.'

He disappeared out the back, his heart thumping and his hands sweaty. Luckily Mick hadn't noticed the exchange, so all was well.

Alex decided to grow a beard. No-one would recognise him then he thought. Joanie thought he looked very handsome with a beard and longed to touch it.

•

When Joanie was eighteen, still plain and still plump, Alex asked Mick for his daughter's hand in marriage.

'Of course my boy, you're part of the family, and I know Joanie is very fond of you. Have you asked her yet?'

'No,' replied Alex. 'I thought it was proper to ask you first.'

'Decent of you Alex, but go ahead. By all means I know she'll be delighted.' He shook Alex's hand. 'Welcome to the family - son.'

That evening Mick retired early explaining that he had a headache. He gave Alex a wink and a nod as he left the room.

'Well, this is it,' Alex thought 'Sink or swim.' Again the ghost of a beautiful red-haired girl flitted through his mind. He brushed it aside.

'Joanie, er, I have something to say to you.'

'Yes, Alex?' She looked up at him, a look of devotion shone in her pale blue eyes.

'Joanie, would you do me the honour of becoming my wife?' He had waited for this moment for many long boring years, but knew it was the only future he could expect. 'Oh yes, oh yes please, Alex.' She flung herself into his arms. As he held her plump little body for the first time he felt no sense of excitement or pleasure. He made himself place a kiss on her cheek.

'Alex, you've made me so happy,' and tears trickled down her face.

'Well, don't cry, I'm sure we'll get on very well,' he added.

Joanie was a little disappointed. He'd said nothing about love, and she had loved him from the moment he had walked into her father's office eight years ago.

'I'll do my best to be a good wife,' she ventured shyly.

'I know you will, Joanie. I'm sure we'll be very happy.' His voice broke, but he hoped his new fiancée didn't realise the real cause of his emotion.

They were to be married in a year, both Mick and Alex agreeing there was no need to hurry the ceremony. Joanie spent the time collecting her trousseau. She made her own clothes, embroidered supper cloths and collected any items she thought she would need.

Her friends were envious – who would have thought plain little Joanie Edwards would marry the best-looking man in town?

'Well, he's not marrying her for her looks,' one of the girls said spitefully. 'Perhaps she has hidden talents.'

They fell into paroxysms of glee. Even in their wildest imagination they couldn't believe plain little Joanie Edwards would do anything naughty.

Alex's love-making consisted of a few hugs and some chaste kisses on her cheek. Mick kept an eagle eye on the young couple and rarely left them alone together. He did not want his daughter to lose her virginity before her wedding, and Alex was not tempted. He treated Joanie with respect and kindness and often wondered if there was any escape from the future he had chosen for himself.

At last they were married but Joanie didn't fall pregnant as everyone had expected. Two years went by, then another one. For Alex making love to his wife was a chore rather than a pleasure, and he wondered if he had made a terrible mistake.

One day Joanie came to him with a happy smile on her face. 'Alex, I have something to tell you.'

'Yes dear,' he said absently, not really paying attention.

'Alex, I'm going to have a baby,' she said shyly.

He looked up startled. 'That's wonderful news, Joanie, that's wonderful.'

He put his arms round her and felt a vague glow of warmth, a warmth that had been mostly missing from his life. Over the years he had learned to control his emotions to such an extent that he went through life feeling neither pain nor joy.

When Joanie had the baby, a chubby little boy, there were complications with the delivery. She lost a great deal of blood and the doctor decided to operate. She nearly died. Alex and Mick were desperately worried. Mick at the thought of losing his precious daughter, and Alex wondering how he could bring up a baby without its mother. It was touch-and-go for a few days, then Joanie started to rally.

She was tearful when Alex visited. 'I'm so sorry,' she whispered, her eyes full of tears.

'Sorry? Why are you sorry? You're going to get better.'

'There won't be any more babies.' And the tears spilled down her cheeks.

'That doesn't matter,' Alex consoled her.

'But I wanted a big family.'

'Well, we have our son, I'm sure he'll be enough to keep you busy.'

'I wondered if we might call him Edward,' she said hesitantly. 'Because Dad doesn't have a son. We could call him Ted.'

'Ted Douglas sounds good to me.'

•

Ted was a difficult baby – he cried a lot – then a difficult boy and grew into a wild young man. Of course Joanie and Mick spoiled him, and when Alex tried to bring him in to line he was outnumbered. Alex had developed into quite a successful business man and ran the stock and station agency with calm efficiency. Mick spent less and less time at the office and more and more time at home with Joanie and Ted. At times Alex felt as if he was living in a prison, one he had created for himself many years before. He would sink in melancholy, and Joanie learned not to worry when he wouldn't speak to her, yelled at their son and shut himself in his room. Neither she nor her father knew what was upsetting Alex.

As he grew older the moods seemed to last longer. The queerer he grew, the more Ted rebelled. He drank too much, he went out with the wrong sort of girl, and didn't seem interested in his father's business. He looked more like his grandfather than his father, and Alex often wondered how he could have fathered a boy whose ways were so alien to his own.

Ted was thirty when his father died. It was a sudden massive heart attack that left Joanie, the elderly Mick and Ted lost and bewildered. Ted pulled himself together. He took over the business, married a lovely girl and produced a son of his own. He in turn had two sons, Alex, named after the grandfather he never knew, and Ted, named after his great-grandfather.

Chapter 6

Rose Louise Gardiner was born in Christchurch, New Zealand, in 1932. It was the time of the Great Depression and the family was very poor. Her father Scott was a school teacher and he was studying to get his Bachelor of Arts degree. Rose was a pretty little baby with bright blue eyes and golden curls. She was a good little baby which was just as well as her mother, Kathleen spent most of her time looking after Rose's older brother, Jimmy. He had rashes and allergies and when he was younger Kathleen carefully bandaged him from top to toe to stop him from scratching. She carried him with one arm while she did her household chores with the other. By means of trial and error, Kathleen found her son was allergic to eggs, fish, nuts and full cream milk.

School teaching had not been Scott's first choice of occupation. He had really wanted to be a farmer but his parents persuaded him against this idea. Firstly because they lacked the finances to support him and secondly they felt he would be better suited to something else. One of his father's friends suggested he might like teaching. He was a charming young man with great communication skills, so when it was found that there was an opening for a junior teacher at the college he was persuaded to accept. It was a school for Maori boys situated not far from where Scott's parents lived in Havelock North in the North Island. Although Scott enjoyed working with the Maori boys he moved from there to teach at a school in New Plymouth. Later still, his career progressed and he moved to Christchurch, where, in fact he had spent his senior years at Christchurch College, the premier boys' school in New Zealand.

Before arriving in Christchurch he married Kathleen, the lovely red-haired daughter of the headmaster of the Napier High School. Then, during their early years of marriage the world became engulfed in the Great Depression. Kathleen, whose father was a frugal man, learned to be even more frugal. In Christchurch the winters were cold and as well as his rashes and allergies Jimmy came down with bronchitis every season.

Scott's father, Reginald, came to the financial rescue when the Depression deepened and the young family moved back to the North Island to Havelock North where he lived.

They moved into the house Ruth and Reginald had built when they returned to New Zealand from Canada, and where Scott had grown up. Reginald was actually born in Australia at Molong where his father, Allen, had been the Church of England Minister. His mother died tragically from a fall from her horse when Reginald was two. Reginald had four older brothers but the oldest in the family was his sister Rose, the only daughter. When his father died in Durban, Reginald was taken by his young stepmother to England where he and his siblings were cared for by his courageous stepmother and his grandmother, affectionately known as Grandma Gardiner, the widow of the famous captain Allen Gardiner. When Reginald's older brother Allen became ill, the family migrated to New Zealand in search of a milder climate.

As a young man, Reginald returned to England for a holiday and met a lovely young French-Canadian girl Ruth Scott. He followed her to Quebec where they married and Scott was born. After the death of a second child, Ruth, Reginald and Scott returned to New Zealand, also in search of warmer weather.

Havelock North was a pretty little village a few miles south of Hastings. Napier was still recovering from an earthquake in 1931 and, as it was only a few miles away, Hastings was going ahead with leaps and bounds.

Scott and his family moved into the house that had been built by his parents when they arrived from Canada and where he had grown up with two younger sisters. Kathleen felt an intruder from the start. Her in-laws had moved to a smaller house next door which was quite comfortable but not as attractive as the home they left. Kathleen had sent messages to her mother-in-law asking her please make sure their milk was from Friesian cows, not the rich Jersey milk. Ruth thought she was being too fussy and didn't bother. After they had been there for a month or so and Jimmy was again covered in a rash from head to foot, Kathleen found they had all been drinking the rich Jersey milk. It was months again before Jimmy's rashes started clearing up. Kathleen never forgave her mother-in-law.

Although they now lived in a lovely house and Scott had a better salary, they were not happy years for the young family. Scott was not teaching. He first of all had been raising money for the Church of England, then the Farmers' Union and was away from the home most of the time. This left Kathleen to face Scott's disapproving parents by herself and with the acute sensitivity that seemed to go with her red hair, she took to heart as criticisms things that were probably meant as kindnesses.

Jimmy attended Hereworth, a primary school for boys and he hated it. On his first day of school Rose went to meet him as he walked home across the paddocks. She was surprised to see him ashen-faced and silent.

'What was it like?' she enquired.

After a while he answered, 'They called me a gutty newbug,' he replied and walked the rest of the way home in silence.

Rose herself didn't fare much better. She attended St Luke's Primary School for girls, that was comprised of two buildings set in the grounds of the local Anglican Church. Rose's aunt taught the youngest children and Miss Budding was in charge of the more senior girls. She quickly recognised Rose's exceptional abilities and encouraged the shy and timid child. However being clever was not considered reason for the girls in her class to like her. One in particular made her life a misery and she used to make up stories to try and impress them. They of course didn't believe her and would shriek with laughter at her pathetic attempts to gain their friendship.

Eventually Scott's two sisters were married. The younger married a local lawyer and the other also married a lawyer and moved to Wellington. Kathleen was so incensed at not being asked to sit at the bridal table with the rest of the family that she refused to go to the second wedding. Rose only realised years later what a hurtful decision this was.

In the meantime Kathleen's father came to live with them and then the Second World War broke out.

They were staying at Tauranga, a town to the north-east from Havelock North for the spring holidays. War was declared a day before Rose's seventh birthday and she was a bit cross that her birthday had been spoiled. However, she was more upset two years later when Kathleen told her that her favourite uncle had been wounded in the fighting against the Germans in the desert. He was one of the Rats of Tobruk and for a short time was held captive by Rommel's forces. Luckily he was rescued, and went on to fight in Greece and Italy but he had a piece of shrapnel in his back for the rest of his life.

Kathleen's father died from pneumonia, as there were no antibiotics at that time. Rose never saw her mother cry or get upset, and her parents never argued or had disagreements. Kathleen controlled the usual fiery temper associated with redheads but turned it inwards upon herself into depression. This was to have a disastrous outcome as she grew older.

In 1942 Scott gained employment as a teacher again, at Nelson College. Nelson was situated in the north of the South Island. Kathleen was delighted, so were Rose and Jimmy. Scott was saddened to notice their relief at the thought of leaving Havelock North, but he was always glad of new opportunities, new places, and new people.

The excited family travelled by train from Hastings to Wellington. In Wellington they caught the overnight ferry to Nelson. The straits between the North and South Islands could be rough, even dangerous. Rose and Jimmy loved every minute of it. Jimmy 'bagsed' the top bunk in their cabin and Rose collapsed with a fit of the giggles as she tickled his feet when he was climbing into it. By morning they had arrived in Nelson. It was a pretty little city, close to the sea to the north and embraced by hills to the east, south, and west.

Having the name Gardiner provided advantages in New Zealand as the family was held in high regard, with friends and acquaintances in many places. Scott had an introduction to the local mayor and his wife, with whom they stayed for a few days while looking for a suitable house to rent. They found one a few blocks from the middle of town, a house nestling into the lower slopes of the Grampian Mountains. The mountains were covered in gorse, a scourge introduced by the early English settlers.

The house which they named 'Whare Kua', meaning 'happy house' in Maori, was but a few blocks from Nelson Boys College. There followed interviews with the headmaster and a few days later Kathleen took Rose to meet Miss Stewart the Headmistress of the Nelson Girls College, situated a few blocks closer to town. Rose was impressed by the size of the buildings, the tennis courts and the swimming pool. Miss Stewart was a large woman of great dignity and a commanding presence.

When their furniture arrived they moved into their new home in Ronaki Terrace. Wandering around as Kathleen and Scott unpacked and placed things in their allotted space, Rose suddenly felt lonely. Everything was strange and different.

'I'm so depressed,' she told her mother and wondered why everyone laughed.

Scott gave her a hug, 'You'll soon feel better,' he comforted. 'How about a cup of tea, Kathleen? You kids can have something to eat, you must be hungry.'

In fact this was the start of the happiest four years of Rose's schooling, even though they were war years and there was rationing of meat, milk, and butter. One dress for good, one for every day, no lollies and chocolates, little petrol and niggling worries about her darling uncle who was still fighting somewhere.

Rose soon made friends at Nelson Girls College. At first, she was in Standard 4, which was housed in a small cottage half a block from the main school. Their teacher was Miss Satchell, nicknamed 'Bags' of course. The girls were friendly and not intimidating, and gradually Rose lost the paralysing shyness that had engulfed her at St Luke's. Her obvious intelligence and ability to excel at anything she did meant that it was soon realised she was a special little girl. Growing more sure of herself, she would pester Miss Satchell with endless questions. Finally she rebuked her. 'Curiosity killed the cat!' she said sarcastically.

Margaret Lewis piped up, 'But it didn't kill Rose.' The girls giggled and Rose felt a glow of happiness.

In Standard 5 they moved to a classroom in the main school. Their teacher was a Miss Burton, an attractive young woman with a lovely singing voice. She raised the parents' ire when she maintained that Dunkirk had been a disaster. The parents were further infuriated when Miss Burton married a man who was a 'conscientious objector'. This did not interfere her teaching skills and, through her, Rose went from strength to strength. She was good at schoolwork, good at sport, loved swimming, cooking and sewing. She loved drawing and went to a special art class. She even had piano lessons although the Gardiners no longer had a piano and she had to go to the neighbours to practice. She also had elocution lessons, and loved every minute of every day.

The summer holidays were a joy. In the morning Rose and Jimmy went swimming at the Boys College baths. The children of the staff were allowed to use them in school holidays. Then in the afternoon Kathleen and Scott took them to the beach. The water was freezing but that didn't matter. When the war started in the Pacific, most of the beach was fenced off with barbed-wire entanglements in the sand hills.

The war in Pacific grew closer and closer. The girls from Nelson Girls College were required to practice air raid drills. For these, they walked to a big old house with an equally old garden and large trees. Here, they were told to huddle beneath the trees which supposedly camouflaged them from the Japanese planes. They thought it was great fun.

Rose wondered why her mother went a pale shade of green when she asked her to sew into her tunic a piece of material with her name, age and address on it. 'It's in case there's an air raid,' Rose told her cheerfully.

Her mother couldn't speak.

Luckily, the war never came to New Zealand. But because of the fighting and the bombing many families – mothers and children – came to New Zealand to escape from war-torn Europe.

In Standard 5 Margaret Jefferies became a welcome addition to Rose and her two friends, Wendy and Judith. Margaret was a plump, plain girl with bright red hair and loads of personality; for some reason she was affectionately known as 'Jimber'. She was soon leader of the pack and by they were all in Standard 6, she was monitor for the primary school. At almost the same time Phillip Corbett and his mother had arrived in Nelson. As a school teacher's pay was only adequate, Kathleen was glad to have Phillip as a boarder when his mother decided to live with relations in the North Island. Phillip was the same age as Jimmy and soon became part of the family.

The year 1945 brought many changes. Rose entered the first year of Senior School. She continued to be top of the class, enjoyed her passion for swimming, cooking and art. In May the war in Europe ended but there were still the Japanese to deal with. New Zealanders had heard about the midget submarines in Sydney Harbour in 1942 but were kept in total ignorance of the fact that northern Australia, including Darwin and Broome, were bombed by the Japanese in the same year. Many Australians did not know about these air raids either, such were the efforts of the Australian Government not to panic the population of the southern states. Then, after the wise or unwise use of the first atomic bombs by the Americans, Japan surrendered.

There was great jubilation. The church bells rang and all the school children were allowed to go into Nelson City to celebrate. There was dancing in the streets and people hugged and kissed perfect strangers. Rose, who was now twelve, thought it would probably be the happiest day of her life. Everyone was laughing or crying. What a day! Rose remembered the feeling of euphoria for the rest of her life.

But there was a downside to the end of the war as there often is to everything. The Nelson College teachers would be returning in 1947.

So far Scott had not been offered a permanent position. Then he heard that the Headmaster of Knox Grammar School in Sydney was in New Zealand interviewing teachers for his prestigious school in Warrawee, an inner north suburb of Sydney. He offered himself for interview.

A few weeks later Scott heard he had indeed been accepted and there was great excitement in the family. 'Going to live in Sydney.' It sounded wonderful, but they were to be bitterly disappointed. Kathleen's health had deteriorated during the war. She had been diagnosed with a problem with her gall bladder, and she was put on a very strict diet. Scott believed she would get better medical attention in Sydney, so they went ahead with their plans to move.

By January 1946 they had packed their clothes, books, and precious things, sold their furniture, given their dog Paddy to friends and were ready for their big adventure. So it was that Scott was taking his sick wife, children but very money to Sydney. The wharf was packed with their friends and well-wishers as they boarded the ferry to Wellington. Rose was too excited to feel sad and her father, ever optimistic, was looking forward to greener pastures. They stayed with Rose's aunt in Wellington, then Scott and Jimmy went to Havelock North to say goodbye to his family. Kathleen refused to go. She needn't have worried; she never saw any of her in-laws again.

They set off in the *Dominion Monarch* for the three-day trip to Sydney. It was a cruise liner that had been converted for carrying troops during the war. The ballroom was covered with hundreds of bunks but the cabins were quite pleasant and the food adequate. Rose and Jimmy were intoxicated with life on board ship. They delighted in seeing the dolphins, which from time to time swam and leapt through the bow waves alongside the ship. The crossing was reasonably calm, even though the Tasman Sea can be treacherous at times, and no-one was seasick.

Early on the fourth day they anchored inside Sydney Harbour and as soon as the ship stopped moving Jimmy disgraced himself by being sick. They looked with awe around the harbour. There were miles and miles and miles of houses. The harbour bridge stood proudly, arching over the vista and Rose could scarcely contain her excitement.

It seemed to take hours for the ship to dock and their luggage to be organised so that they could go ashore. As they stepped ashore a blast of hot humid air engulfed them. It was 104 degrees Fahrenheit and very sticky. Years later, they would all still feel waves of depression pass over them on the first really hot day of summer.

After the shock of the heat there was another disaster. Scott thought the headmaster had promised them suitable accommodation when they arrived in Sydney. But had he? There was none waiting apparently. There was nowhere for them to go.

A friend of the Gardiner family drove them to Knox Grammar School where the headmaster had grudgingly said they could stay in the school hospital for a few days. Rose marvelled at the rows and rows of houses, suburb after suburb on the North Shore line. 'Look at all the brick chimneys!' she exclaimed. 'You'd think they'd all come down if there was an earthquakes.'

'They don't have earthquakes here,' Jimmy announced condescendingly. 'Oh.'

Growing up in the 'shaky isles', they were all used to a little rattling and shaking. Kathleen was terrified of earthquakes but luckily hadn't implanted the same fear in her children. Rose used to get cross if they happened in the night and she didn't wake up.

They eventually arrived at Warrawee and climbed out of the car, carrying their suitcases and feeling sadly disillusioned. This was not the welcome they had expected. A kindly housekeeper showed them where they were to stay. There was no sign of the headmaster.

The first item on the agenda was to obtain ration books. For these they had to venture into the city, so the next morning they set out, bravely catching the train and hoping they would know the right place to get off.

Rose was staggered by the people, the shops, the trams and the heat. They returned to their inadequate lodgings with the necessary ration cards in hand, but exhausted and deflated.

A few days later Kathleen was moved to a room in an old people's home in Wahroonga, the same suburb as Rose's new school, Abbotsleigh. Jimmy was to stay with a friend of a friend, and Scott would live at Knox until they found a home.

The old people's home was run by a grumpy lady who mistreated the old people in her care. Rose would never forget the mournful cries of the local birds, and the disappointment of their great adventure turning to dust. Then another blow fell. Jimmy was hoping to go to university in Australia, but the New Zealand accredited matriculation was not accepted and he would have to sit two subjects, Latin and English, and pass these exams before he would be accepted.

Rose started school at Abbotsleigh. It was a prestigious school with a wonderful academic record. It was attended by the daughters of the rich and famous, gleaned from the wealthy North Shore suburbs, and wealthy graziers from all parts of New South Wales. Rose had not been able to obtain a proper uniform as the shops still suffered from wartime shortages.

She felt uncomfortable, out of place, and terribly homesick, what with the heat, the torture of living in a strange new land, among strange new people. Rose became ill with a mysterious illness and missed two or three weeks of school. Kathleen's health was deteriorating too and she was rushed in to hospital to have her gall bladder removed. The doctors found that it was in fact a badly infected appendix that had attached itself to her gall bladder and only removed the appendix. Years later she did develop gall bladder problems but by then the doctors couldn't operate because of her bad heart.

Scott stayed with Rose at the old people's home and three weeks later brought his wife home from hospital, a tiny shadow of her former self.

Finally, there was some good news. The headmaster had found a place for them to stay in Warrawee, close to both schools. They had to share with an elderly lady who seemed pleasant enough to begin with but was to prove to be rather neurotic

Jimmy found a job working in a paper store in the city and at last they were all together again. Rose started to come out of her shell and enjoyed the company of the smart, sophisticated girls who were her class mates. She was soon included in their social functions. There were parties every weekend, tennis parties, evening parties with boys from Knox, Barker and other schools. The girls now had a dress for every party, wore make-up and high-heeled shoes. Rose had one dress her mother had made. She had flat shoes and refused to wear make-up. Gradually her shyness disappeared and she began to enjoy herself. Then the results of her first term at Abbotsleigh came out. She was appalled. She had come fifteenth in the class! Having been top of her class in every subject all her school life Rose felt humiliated and ashamed.

However, the next term, when the weather was cooler, her spirits lifted and she worked very hard. She came top of the class. But then the family had to move again. Their neurotic lady became even more neurotic and asked them to leave. Kathleen had come down with pneumonia and seemed very frail, but with a hopeful heart she went about packing their things and trying to make the best of a dismal situation.

They moved to Pymble where they were to share a flat with a man who had just lost his wife. However, he would not be there often and apart from being melancholy he was, at least, a gentle man.

The flat was in a large old house that had been converted into six flats. They had an upstairs flat which had wonderful views towards the city. There were really only two bedrooms. Rose slept in a tiny room, just large enough for a single bed that unfortunately was situated above all the bathrooms of the downstairs flats. All night she would hear toilets flushing. The weather grew warmer, her school work deteriorated and finally Scott decided enough was enough and he applied for a job at The Armidale School, a private boys school founded in 1894. Armidale was three hundred or so miles north of Sydney on the New England tablelands. It was a small city of 8000 but it boasted two cathedrals, great schools and a university college. The climate was a great attraction as, high on the tablelands, its summers were cool and dry, its winters had frosts and even occasional falls of snow.

It sounded like bliss. There were two well-known girls' schools in Armidale: the New England Girls School – NEGS – which was run by the Anglican Church and Presbyterian Ladies College – PLC. NEGS only took boarders, so Rose went PLC. It was a small school with under one hundred students whom she found to be vastly different from their city cousins. The boarders were simple, unsophisticated and uncomplicated country girls and the day girls were mainly daughters of local businessmen. They were friendly and kind and Rose wasn't afflicted by the shyness and vulnerability she had when she first went to Abbotsleigh.

It was now 1947 and there was a great lack of teachers for country schools and so the girls were taught French by the French master of the boys' school, TAS. Rose was taught Ancient History by her father at home and, as she was the only girl who studied Latin, she would visit a Miss Harris in once a week. Having a problem with her back Miss Harris wore a plaster cast and had difficulty moving – thus the home visits. A downside to the little friendly school was that for the next three years Rose didn't really have to exert her brain to come top of every subject. Abbotsleigh, in spite of all its faults and the family's dire accommodation problems, had widened her horizons, stimulated her brain and made her think.

Jimmy went to the University College to study for a Bachelor of Arts degree. It was a college of Sydney University and there were only two or three hundred students. Jimmy enjoyed university life and soon made friends. They were a happy-go-lucky lot, not too serious, but not too wild.

The family settled into a comfortable little cottage in Mann Street. It was south of the town but only a few blocks from the centre and even in the middle of summer, was not too hot. During the summer, the town often seemed to get a shower and a storm every afternoon. It seemed like paradise after the heat and humidity of Sydney.

The year in Sydney had taken its toll on Kathleen and Scott. They were thrilled that Jimmy could at last go to university but didn't pay much attention to Rose's opportunities. Scott rushed off and bought a piano but Rose did not have any more piano lessons. She taught herself to play easy bits of classical music and to play the current pop songs. She loved playing the piano, and didn't question the lack of lessons.

Scott seemed to have lost his sense of humour and didn't regale the family with jokes and funny stories as he had done in Nelson. Kathleen's health was fragile, both physically and mentally, and it didn't take much to push her over the edge a few years later.

Why hadn't they returned to New Zealand when things had gone so badly for them in Sydney? Rose pondered this dilemma for the rest of her life. Was it pride, or lack of money for the fares? Rose never knew.

After three years she completed her education as dux of the school. Jimmy graduated with his Arts degree and went to work for the local paper, the *Armidale Express* as a journalist. This had always been his ambition.

Nobody took much notice of Rose's ambitions and she couldn't remember her parents ever discussing the subject with her. She was offered a job in a local business which handled real estate insurance. She answered the phone, wrote out receipts and occasionally wrote letters for the boss. After completing only half a typing and shorthand course at the local convent, Rose thought she could do both well enough to get by. She was bored stiff. What was the girl who had the highest IQ Nelson Girls College had ever known doing menial tasks in an office?

Jimmy and Rose enjoyed the social life that Armidale offered its young people, although it wasn't as sophisticated as the social life she had experienced at the age of fourteen in Sydney. She met the family of Margaret, her best friend at school. Margaret invited her to stay with them out in the bush just after Ruth left school. They lived on a property at Glenfoyle, seventy miles north-east of Armidale on the Guyra-Ebor road. Margaret had an older brother, Bill, a charming and handsome young man.

On a visit, Margaret introduced Rose to her parents, Johnny and Mary Harrison. They seemed a lot older than Rose's parents, which indeed they were. They lived in an old weatherboard house, which, in Rose's eyes, looked shabby and dilapidated. Goodness me, thought Rose, I thought Margaret came from a family of wealthy graziers. She was welcomed kindly by Mary and shown to her room by Margaret.

'When you've settled in we'll have a nice cup of tea,' Mary suggested.

'Thank you Mrs Harrison. That will be lovely.'

The house was surrounded by verandahs on every side. A hall led into the kitchen and then the dining room. In the centre was a passage leading to the bathroom, Margaret and her parents' bedrooms. Through the lounge to the south of the verandah were two more bedrooms, the first was the guest room, the second Bill's bedroom.

Rose unpacked her suitcase and hung up a couple of dresses she had brought with her. Then she and Margaret joined the others in the kitchen for the promised cup of tea. It was not a large room but had an open fire, a fuel stove and a kerosene refrigerator.

'We don't have mains electricity,' Margaret explained. 'We have thirty-two volt engine that has to be run every evening so that we can have electric lights. It often breaks down and then we use kerosene lamps.'

The walls were grimy with smoke and Rose thought it was just as well the light wasn't very good.

'Would you like to freshen up?' Mary enquired. 'Margaret will show you where the bathroom is.'

Dutifully Rose followed her friend along the middle passage. She noticed there was something important missing from the bathroom. There was no lavatory.

They sat down to a wonderful afternoon tea at which there was a sponge, a gingerbread loaf and some tasty biscuits. Rose loved sponge cakes, and this one was filled with the most gorgeous thick cream.

'This is delicious!' she exclaimed.

'My mother is a very good cook,' Margaret agreed proudly.

'So are you, Margaret,' her mother added.

After the magnificent afternoon tea Margaret suggested she show Rose around the garden. They walked out the back door and down the path at the end of which there was a gate into a paddock that held the laundry and clothes lines.

It was when they went through the gate that Rose realised the purpose of the 'look around'. A few yards to the south was the 'little house'.

'We call it the long drop,' Margaret laughed. 'If you want to go I'll keep guard,' she said mischievously.

'Oh thanks, yes I will,' Rose mumbled.

Inside there was a seat above a very long drop, and a very bad smell.

How can people still live like this? she wondered.

Apart from the lavatory arrangements, they had a very happy few days. Bill was kind and attentive. Rose and Margaret had been best friends at school and often collapsed in fits of giggles over nothing in particular.

Bill took the girls for a picnic 'down the paddock'. The property stretched a few miles to the north where it stopped abruptly by dropping some 2000 feet to the gulf country below. When they drove round the hill which prevented the family from seeing this view from their home, Rose saw row upon row of hills stretching in the distance.

Thank goodness, Rose thought. They might not be snow-capped mountains but at least they were hills.

'On a clear day you can see Queensland,' Bill announced cheerfully.

Margaret giggled. 'They say? Who's they? Has anyone ever proved it?'

'Well, I don't suppose you could,' Bill admitted.

They drove down on rough bush tracks. Most of the country to the north was still covered in gum trees although he paddocks closer to home had been cleared.

Bill found a pleasant spot to park near a creek, and they settled on rugs, brought out the food and a thermos of tea and admired the view and the peace and quiet.

'I thought you would have boiled a billy,' Rose commented in a slightly sarcastic tone.

'A billy!' Bill laughed. 'Come on, Rose. We don't live back in the dark ages.'

Rose felt like saying that their lack of plumbing was just that, but was careful not to say it.

Then Bill said quietly, 'Rose, don't move, and don't look behind you.' He quietly picked up a stick and hit something on the ground just behind Rose. She looked around and was horrified to see a snake, writhing and turning. In a few minutes it was still.

Rose shrieked and stood up. 'Oh, my goodness, a snake. I've never seen a snake before.' She was trembling.

'It's okay, it's only a blackie,' Bill said calmly. 'Black snakes will give you a nasty bite but they won't kill you.'

'Thanks very much.' Rose was still trembling.

Margaret laughed at her friend's distress. 'It's the brown snakes, the copperheads, that will kill you.'

'Come on Margaret, don't tease the poor girl. You know you don't see them very often,' Bill said.

'Not round the house, but there are plenty down the paddocks,' Margaret retorted. 'Having frightened our visitor half to death, I think it's time we went home.'

Rose laughed nervously. 'Well, that certainly made my day.'

Over the next few months Bill, Rose, Jimmy and Margaret made a happy foursome. They went to the show, the picnic races, the Country Party younger set dances, and if there was nothing else on they went to the pictures on Saturday nights. Jimmy was quite taken with Rose's friend as she was a very pretty girl with dark hair, brown flashing eyes and a deadly sense of humour. Jimmy and Bill also got on well together and for the first time since the family had left New Zealand, Rose felt a measure of happiness.

Kathleen and Scott also liked Bill and Margaret. In fact, Kathleen thought Bill was very suitable company for her young daughter. After all he was a wealthy grazier and good- looking too.

Some months after Rose had visited Glenfoyle, Bill suddenly developed suspected appendicitis. As his father drove him to Armidale hospital, Bill insisted that his father stop the car outside Rose's house so that he could see her for a few moments. Rose leaned in the window and held his hand. She was shocked, he looked so pale.

'Good luck Bill,' Rose whispered, 'I'll be thinking of you.'

And then they were gone.

Bill soon recovered from the immediate effects of the operation, but his doctor did not want him to return to the bush for a few weeks in case he tried to go back to work too soon. Kathleen kindly offered to look after him when he was discharged from hospital. She had done some nursing training after leaving school when she was nineteen but had not finished the course as she had to return home to nurse her dying mother and look after her two young brothers.

When Bill arrived from hospital to stay with the Gardiners his pale and drawn face tugged at Rose's heart. Kathleen was in her element, fussing over Bill, cooking him nourishing meals and making sure he didn't exert himself too much, but it was Rose's sweet smile that brought the colour back to his cheeks and the sparkle to his eyes.

After a week or so Bill's parents rang to ask when he was coming home, but Kathleen insisted he still wasn't strong enough to go back to work.

Finally Johnny Harrison grew more than impatient and told Kathleen bluntly that he would come for Bill the very next day. He was tucked up in bed when Rose went in to say good night. She held his hand. As well as Kathleen, she had enjoyed spoiling him. She had a feeling he did not get much affection at home. His mother Mary was a very undemonstrative woman; Rose never saw her show any signs of affection to her family.

'It's been lovely having you here,' Rose murmured. 'I'm going to kiss you.'

Bill tightened the hold on her hand. He was obviously desperate to say something to her but just couldn't get it out.

'What is it, Bill?' she asked.

Finally the words tumbled out. 'Rose, Rose, I love you. Will you marry me?'

Rose was stunned. She didn't know what to say.

'Please, Rose.' Bill pleaded.

She was very fond of him, and all her family liked him. Rose had made no progress with what she might do with her life – nobody wanted to talk about it. Perhaps *this* was her destiny. She could give Bill the love and affection he did not get from his family. After all, she had been looking after her mother off and on since she was sixteen. In spite of her many talents, perhaps to love someone was her best gift.

'Yes, I will Bill,' she said.

They hugged. Both were crying.

'We won't tell anyone for a little while,' Rose suggested.

Bill agreed, and next morning Johnny and Mary duly arrived and whisked their errant son back to the bush, back to work. Kathleen noticed a bemused look on Rose's face over the next few days. 'Is there anything you want to tell me?' she gently enquired.

Rose flushed deep pink and stammered, 'Well yes I guess, I mean… Bill asked me to marry him.'

'And you said yes?' Kathleen asked, fairly sure of the answer

Rose nodded. 'But we're not telling anyone for a while.'

Kathleen knew Rose meant Bill's parents in particular. She agreed. 'That's a good idea, it might be a good idea to wait until your eighteen, but I'm so happy. Bill's a lovely young man. I'm sure you'll be very happy with him.'

After her life with Scott and his spasmodic income, plus his urge to move every few years, Kathleen thought a settled life with a wealthy grazier would be perfect for her daughter, never mind that Rose was only seventeen and had the brains and ability to do almost anything she wished.

Rose and Bill were engaged for a long eighteen months. Mary and Johnny did not approve of their sons choice – she wasn't a country girl. What was the use of book learning and school teaching when you lived in the bush? They delayed getting a builder to construct a house for the young couple, secretly hoping the whole thing would fall through before they needed to spend any money on that. All that Mary said to Rose when she heard of the engagement was, 'I hope you haven't gone off the deep end and regret it for the rest of your life.' Not much of a welcome to the family.

Kathleen's health suddenly deteriorated. On top of which, the ladies who renting them the house in Mann Street to the Gardiner family suddenly decided they wanted to live in it themselves. Good rental accommodation was hard to find in Armidale as university and teacher's college students occupied most of it.

Kathleen, who had always been so self-controlled, went to pieces. Rose had never seen her mother cry, never heard her parents argue or even be impatient with each other. The arrival of menopause, a matter which was never mentioned in the 1950s, added to her mental problems that had been caused by the terrible year in Sydney.

Kathleen started to cry inexplicably all the time. She cried for a year. Scott simply switched off as he didn't know how to handle a tearful wife. Jimmy spent most of his time out with his university friends, so it was left to Rose to look after her mother. She did this with enormous patience, sweetness and loving kindness.

Finally the Harrisons engaged a builder to start work on a house for Bill and Rose. Rose planned the house herself, but her future father-in-law said it was much too big and they would have to cut out one of the bedrooms and reduce the size of the lounge room.

Then another blow fell. Kathleen, after claiming that Bill was the answer to a maiden's prayer, suddenly decided she didn't like him. In fact she developed an immovable loathing for him and she would spend the next fifteen years being nasty to him whenever the opportunity arose.

Jimmy and Margaret, who had been courting, split up. Rose was marrying into a family who didn't like her, and now her best friend didn't like her either.

Kathleen's health improved enough for her to organise and attend the wedding. With a double mortgage, Scott and Kathleen bought a little house just outside Armidale. Scott could no longer wander round the country as he had done in the past as his wife was too ill to move again.

Rose and Bill moved into an unfurnished house. There were four rooms with windows: a kitchen, a dining room, a bedroom and a bathroom. The house had been built by a pleasant young man, Freddie who later married Margaret.

Luckily for Rose, during the first six months of married life, Bill helped Freddie complete the house so she had plenty of company. When the house was finished, Bill returned to working on the property. He mostly drove a tractor but would help with the stock work when there was crutching or shearing sheep or branding cattle.

•

Rose threw herself into the life of a country wife with enthusiasm. She had always loved cooking, having made cakes and biscuits for her mother's afternoon parties from as early as twelve. Bill loved growing vegetables and he planted an orchard which soon produced a variety of fruits. Rose bought a Vacola bottling outfit and in the summer bottled peaches, nectarines and plums to eat during the winter. She made pickles with green tomatoes, relish with red ones, jam with blackberries that grew wild on the property, apricots, and had to buy citrus to make marmalade.

But the days were long and lonely. The Harrisons didn't have many friends, just relations – of which there were plenty. Mary came from a large family and Bill had uncles, aunts, and cousins by the score. They all seemed to live on properties and Rose felt uncomfortable at the family gatherings, given to wondering if she would ever fit in and become a part of the Aussie bush.

Jimmy had met a girl, Kerry, who was on a working holiday around Australia. She came from Melbourne and once they became engaged, he decided to go to Melbourne with her to further his career in journalism. Because of Jimmy's absence, Kathleen decided there was nothing in her life worth living for and took to her bed. Although she had a devoted husband and a loving daughter, without her son she didn't want to do anything. She had developed a heart problem, angina. On top of this, she developed a rash for which she had to have cortisone injections and some time later really did have a problem with her gall bladder.

Rose and Bill did not feel they were in any hurry to have children. Rose found it difficult to become pregnant as she had a retroverted uterus. Finally, three years after they were married, Stuart was born.

Kathleen took one look at the dear little baby boy and bounced out of bed. At last there was another little boy who could replace Jimmy in her heart. She spoilt him rotten, much to Bill's disgust. Even with this new attraction and an apparent new lease of life, Kathleen had not recovered from her mental problems, would cry frequently, developed agoraphobia and wouldn't leave the house except to visit Rose and Bill and Stuart.

As the years went by, two daughters, Jane and Louise, arrived to complete the family. Bill and Rose adored their daughters.

When he was old enough, Rose had to take Stuart to school at Wongwibinda, five miles from their home. This was the start of did school runs she did for thirteen years but she was still devastated each time she had to send them, one by one, to boarding school in Armidale. Stuart went to The Armidale School when he was twelve.

The whole family were all away at the coast for the May school holidays when Kathleen had a massive stroke and died. Despite the trials he had lived through with Kathleen, Scott was inconsolable and decided to go back to New Zealand to live. Rose bid him a tearful farewell, and wondered what she would do with herself without either parent to look after. But she need not have worried. After two years Scott suffered a heart attack and when he regained his strength, he came back to live with Rose and her family. The little girls were still at home, and even though Stuart was at boarding school, Rose could see that the children got on her father's nerves. It was probably because of this, he bought a house at

Sawtell on the coast and proposed to spend the odd weekend there. The weekend stretched into weeks, then months. He enjoyed life at the coast, the people were friendly and his health seemed to improve. However, in church at Repton one Sunday, he had another heart attack and died.

Rose was shocked beyond belief. Her brother Jimmy was living in Melbourne. He had married Kerry and they had two children, but Rose had rarely seen him since he had left Armidale. She felt so alone, surrounded by Bill's relatives and his less-than-loving family.

But by the time the three children were all at boarding school, Rose and Bill found themselves making friends with other parents, and their social life gradually improved. In a few years they were being asked out to lunch nearly every weekend or entertaining friends themselves. So much so that they bought a beautiful mahogany dining table which seated eighteen, and with her love of cooking undiminished, Rose enjoyed preparing feasts for her guests.

Over the years, they had built two extra bedrooms so that the girls and Stuart would have a bedroom each. Inevitably the girls' rooms were empty once they went to board at New England Girls School. However, it was not long before Stuart had finished his schooling and returned home to help his father run the property. His parents had tried to persuade him to go to university, but no, all he wanted to do was come home and work on the land that he loved. With his father's help and encouragement, he took over the stock work, while Bill still drove the tractor, clearing land and sowing pastures.

Rose had dreaded taking the girls back to school after the holidays. It made the house seem so quiet and empty. Now, after being involved in journeys to and from and in school functions for many years it was quite a shock to her when the time came that they had all left school. True, Stuart came home, but the girls didn't. Jane went to the teachers college in Armidale and gained her Diploma of Education. But teaching positions were hard to find and she went to Sydney, took a rapid secretarial course and obtained a very good job with Price Waterhouse, a firm of accountants. Louise was already in Sydney, training to be a Tresillian nurse, looking after babies. They shared flats with friends, first in Bondi then in succession in Paddington, Mosman and Glebe. On completing her training, Louise was employed as a nurse in charge to babies up to two-year-olds at the Redfern Day Care Centre.

Rose loved going to Sydney to visit her daughters while Bill went on fishing trips to the Great Barrier Reef and the Gulf of Carpentaria. She would go shopping at Double Bay, go to shows and the ballet, and saw *Cats*, *Phantom of the Opera* and *Les Miserables*.

As the years went by they went through droughts to floods, through good prices for their wool and cattle and through bad prices. Life on the land was not the safe haven Rose had expected it to be.

Chapter 7

With the girls settled and earning their own living, and Stuart capable of running the property by himself, Rose and Bill decided to do some travelling. They had made a few trips to New Zealand, where Rose visited her relations and Bill loved to fish. They decided to venture further afield. Rose decided she must have inherited the Gardiner wanderlust as she liked nothing better than planning the next trip when they had just returned from the last one.

They chose a cruise to Fiji, Vanuatu and Tonga to begin with. This was not a success for although they loved seeing the people and customs of different islands, Rose was seasick almost as soon as they left Sydney Harbour and they were both terribly sick on their way home from Fiji.

'No more cruises,' Rose decided.

The next expedition was much more exciting. They flew to Canada where Rose's darling uncle after whom she had named Stuart, lived in Victoria on Vancouver Island. This was a lovely ferry trip from Vancouver. After a few days with her aunt and uncle they joined a bus trip through the Rockies. The magnificence of the scenery captivated Rose. Here there were snow-capped mountains in abundance, even though it was midsummer. Then they flew to San Francisco where they joined another group of Australians. They made their way to Los Angeles, flew to Las Vegas for the day, flew over the Grand Canyon, visited Mexico and had a couple of days in Hawaii on their way home.

Their new trip was even more adventurous. They toured the United Kingdom, then the continent, and were away for nearly three months.

They returned to Canada, again visited with Rose's uncle then cruised from Vancouver to Skagway, stopping at Ketchican and Juneau in Alaska. The inside passage was as calm as a mill pond, and Rose loved every minute of it. From Skagway they bussed back into northern Canada then to Fairbanks and the Benali National Park where they saw grizzly bears and went white water rafting. On to Anchorage, then to Valdez where they boarded a ship to travel Prince William Sound a spot which was later to devastated by an oil spill.

Another wonderful trip they undertook was to Kenya, stopping at Singapore and Mauritius on the way. They stayed in several game parks, including Tree Tops where Princess Elizabeth received the news of her father death and that she had become Queen.

Rose and Bill were enchanted by the animals in Kenya. It was exciting and a little frightening driving in their special bus close to a herd of elephants, stopping some distance from a pride of lions which were lazily sleeping in the sun. The giraffes were enchanting and the thousands of zebra and wildebeest on the Masai Mara was an incredible experience.

They visited Hong Kong and China. In spite of seeing the Great Wall, the Forbidden City in Beijing and the Terracotta Warriors, this was the bottom of Rose's list as she picked up a nasty stomach infection in Xian. Bill, on the other hand, loved every minute of the trip to China.

They had become seasoned travellers and this was Rose's intention for she had two more trips in mind, more exacting and even more dangerous than any they had been on before. She wanted to follow in the footsteps of her great-great-grandfather Captain Allen Gardiner, first to Durban and then to Tierra del Fuego. When her father died Rose had found a box marked 'Gardiner Family History' and in it she found many treasures.

She had never heard her father talk about Captain Gardiner, but her mother had told her: 'He was an officer in the Royal Navy and became a missionary. He died on the shores of Tierra del Fuego.'

Not willing to admit that she had no idea where Tierra del Fuego was, she asked no more. In the box was a book of poems written by Captain Gardiner and a book of pencil sketches he had made of different places to which he had travelled when he was a naval officer. There were several books written about his exploits and two written by Captain Gardiner himself about a trip to South Africa, and another about crossing South America from Buenos Aires, over the Andes to Chile with his second wife and children.

Rose became engrossed in and fascinated by the life of her ancestor. She determined that she and Bill would go to the places he had been and Bill was almost as enthusiastic as she was. In case it turned out to be a disappointment and that no-one would be interested in their arrival, she told her friends they were going to Perth for a holiday. Her family was sworn to secrecy. She and Bill did fly to Perth of course, but only stayed there for a couple of hours waiting to board the plane to Harare, the capital of Zimbabwe. Their travel agent had told them there was only one hotel to stay in Harare and that it was beautiful. They were warned however, on their arrival not to venture out of the hotel, not even to the park opposite.

Rose gazed out their window. 'It doesn't look very dangerous. There just seems to be some people selling carved animals.'

'Let's go and have a look.'

'Okay.'

There were wooden animals of all shapes and sizes, tall giraffes, lions, monkeys, hippos, every African animal you could think of, and their owners desperately trying to sell Rose and Bill anything, at any price. They settled on a chunky hippo which had a nice smile and scuttled back to their hotel in case something terrible did happen.

Next day they made their way to the Victoria Falls, where they stayed in a nearby hotel. There were tourists everywhere, meandering along bush tracks, looking for their first sight of the falls. It was a wondrous sight and worth every minute of their scary night in Harare.

The next day they flew to Johannesburg where they had to change flights and board another plane for Durban. Johannesburg airport was in chaos; there had been some extreme weather overnight, even a fall of snow on the Brackensburg Mountains. All flights were delayed, some even cancelled. Rose and Bill settled in for a long wait. Finally they thought their flight number was called. They presented their tickets and were given boarding passes. Eventually they were allowed on to the plane and ushered to their seats toward the back of the aircraft. They heard the engines revving for takeoff when one of the air hostesses approached them.

'Mr and Mrs Harrison, I'm afraid you are on the wrong flight, every flight is so delayed, yours doesn't actually leave for another hour.'

Feeling foolish, Rose and Bill stood up to collect their belongings. 'We are actually taking off right now,' the air hostess explained, 'but I'm afraid your luggage isn't. You will have to wait for it when you get to Durban.'

Rose and Bill sat down in some confusion. 'I thought you weren't allowed to fly if your luggage wasn't on the plane,' Rose murmured.

'So did I.'

'How do they know we're not terrorists?'

'They don't,' Bill laughed. 'Don't worry, Rose. I'm sure everything is going to be okay.'

'Well, I'm not,' Rose replied, crossly.

Because of the storms, the plane was bucked around, suddenly dropping and shaking. Rose clutched the seat in front of her. She remembered seeing in one of the books about Captain Gardiner, a remark in her father's handwriting, 'Brave or foolish.' She didn't usually feel nervous in aeroplanes - hated airports, loved flying.

'Brave or foolish?' she whispered.

'What did you say?' Bill asked.

She repeated it a little louder. 'Are we being brave or foolish?'

'Brave of course.' There was a hint of amusement in Bill's voice. He squeezed Rose's hand. 'Come on, old girl. We're just going through a bit of turbulence. We'll soon be in Durban safe and sound.'

'I don't know, perhaps it's all a mistake. Perhaps....'

'Nonsense.'

They were met by Nancy, a charming and lively public relations lady, who seemed quite unperturbed that they would have to wait for their luggage to arrive. Rose had written to the local Historical Society, the Church of England, the Durban newspapers, and several others telling them of her connection with Captain Gardiner and the reason for their visit.

Nancy was a bundle of energy and drove them to their hotel and explained the plans for the next day.

The Royal was a beautiful hotel right in the middle of the city and as Rose sank on to the luxurious bed she exclaimed, 'Well, Captain Allen, we're here!'

Next morning they met Nancy who was full of enthusiasm and pleased with her research into the Gardiner family. 'I have found your great-grandfather grave,' she announced. 'It is in the old cemetery and is sadly neglected I'm afraid. Luckily it's not far away so I thought we would go there now.'

Rose felt sad as she looked at the headstone crumbling with disrepair and neglect over a hundred years. She realised she was the first member of the Gardiner family to see it since the Reverend Allen Gardiner's second wife and younger children had left Durban, returning to England with Grandma Gardiner, the widow of Captain Allen, and Reverend Allen's older children.

'Thank you for finding him,' Rose murmured.

'Well, my dears, I think we'll go to the cathedral where he served for just a few short weeks.'

Rose was surprised to find the Reverend Allen Gardiner's name in the church at the top of the list of incumbent clergymen. He had been so determined to follow in his father's footsteps but had died from malaria only a few short weeks after arrival in Durban;

Nancy could feel the air of sadness settling on Rose and Bill. 'Come, I have another church to show you, then we might drive down to the park for lunch.'

The other church was a little chapel situated in Julia Street. The street had been named after Captain Gardiner's daughter, Julia, who had died just as he arrived in Durban with his second wife and children to further pursue his missionary work.

Julia's headstone stood in the grounds of the chapel although she wasn't buried here. The vicar explained that her headstone had been found elsewhere and placed here as a memorial. Inside the chapel there was a coloured-glass window portraying Captain Gardiner preaching to an assembly of parishioners. Tears came to Rose's eyes. She hadn't been prepared for the overwhelming emotions she felt when faced with these poignant reminders of her ancestors.

Before they had lunch, Nancy showed them the bust of Captain Allen Gardiner, 'Founder of Durban', in Gardiner Street, the main street.

By the end of the day Rose felt emotionally and physically exhausted.

'You look done in,' Bill sympathised. 'Perhaps we'd better have a spell tomorrow.'

'No, we're meeting the members of the Historical Society, and I think I'm expected to give a talk,' Rose reminded him

The next day the phone started ringing. The local newspaper wanted to do an interview and a lady from the museum, which contained many books and memorabilia about the famous Captain, insisted they visit. A local schoolteacher rang to say that her class were learning about Julia and her father. 'You are brave coming here,' she told Rose.

Brave? She hadn't realised quite how brave she needed to be. After the interview with the press, an article appeared reporting that she was the first descendant of Captain Gardiner in over a hundred years to honouring Durban with her presence. It also published her photograph.

Rose and Bill visited the museum, and although they were rather worried that the taxi driver was taking so long to get there, they were greeted with kindness and enthusiasm by Helen, the curator. There were so many things of interest that she showed them. She offered to drive them up into the hills the next day so that they could see the countryside and arranged to pick them up at their hotel.

The hotel had two entrances and, of course, Rose and Bill waited at the wrong one. Eventually the doorman appeared. 'Mr and Mrs Harrison, there is a lady waiting for you at the other entrance. She asks that you be as quick as you can as she is worried about being car-napped.'

Hastily they found Helen's car and apologised to her. They were discovering white people could have difficulty in the formerly apartheid-governed Durban.

It was a very pleasant drive into the hills and away from the city. At lunch they met a friend of Helen's who was writing a book about the early pioneers. This of course included a chapter of Captain Gardiner.

On their way back, they realised they would be late for an appointment with one of the members from the Historical Society. Helen offered to ring and explain that they would be late. They stopped at a little shopping centre, but a few minutes later Helen returned ashen-faced. 'I couldn't use the phone,' she said. 'There was a murder there yesterday and it wasn't safe.'

They rang when they had returned to their hotel. 'You know, Bill, if I'd realised it was going to be so....'

'So dangerous, you mean? You wouldn't have come,' he teased.

'Of course I'd have come,' she replied enthusiastically, 'I'm not Captain Allen's great-great-granddaughter for nothing you know!'

'That's the spirit. Onward and upward – that's what I think.'

They hugged. 'I think I need a drop of whisky, just to warm me up. Like a brandy, my love?'

'Yes please.'

The next day was of great importance to Rose. Two local historians, Judith and Stephen Middleton, took them to the place where Dingarn, the bloodthirsty Zulu chieftain had lived over 150 years before. Dingarn's kraal was a two hour trip from Durban. This was where he had lived with hundreds, possibly thousands, of Zulu warriors.

They were to travel by car and Rose wondered why Judith and Stephen seemed a little nervous when they arrived at the hotel. Rose put some things on the bonnet of the car. Quickly Stephen picked them up and handed them back to Rose. 'Never leave things, always make sure your possessions are safe.' Stephen sounded irritable and upset with the day's proceedings already.

'I'm sorry I didn't mean....' Rose's voice trailed away. It occurred to her that anything was likely to happen at any time. Rose felt guilty at asking these kind people to do something that was obviously fraught with danger. They set off, and once away from the city Judith and Stephen seemed to relax.

The roads were good; there was little traffic as they sped north and west of Durban. Judith had packed lunch for them and after about an hour they stopped at a village. They sat in a little park, and in the distance a group of local villagers gathered. They were neither friendly nor unfriendly, just curious.

After hastily eating Judith's sandwiches and drinking tea from her thermos, they were quickly on their way again. There was little conversation in the car and Rose felt more and more uncomfortable that she had expected these kind people to do something which was quite perilous.

The countryside was empty of habitation but attractive with rolling hills of green. 'We're nearly there,' Stephen announced. 'They are turning the place where Dingarn had his kraal site into a historical site.'

There was small building at the entrance to the site where Stephen paid in order to be permitted to enter to area.

'You may drive where you wish,' the lady at entrance told them, 'At the moment we are reconstructing huts similar to the ones in which Dingarn and his warriors lived.'

They drove slowly over the uneven ground and then saw the huts.

'We'll have a look at them,' Stephen said. He stopped the car and they all disembarked. As if by magic another car drew up, and two men quickly came towards them. One was black, the other white. The white man carried an expensive camera. 'Good morning,' he said.

'Good morning,' they replied in unison.

'We've been told, that is we've heard…' The black man paused. 'We've been told that a descendant of Captain Allen Gardiner is to be here today.' He looked at them anxiously.

'Well, yes, that's me,' Rose exclaimed.

'We're very pleased to meet you.' There were handshakes all round.

'He was my great-great-grandfather,' Rose explained, 'and I'm trying to follow in his footsteps, and I know he spent some time here Dingarn.'

'He certainly did and if you would like to look in this hut, we know it is in the exact place that Dingarn had his hut because we found beads buried in the ground. Only the king of the Zulus would have lived there. Would you like to go inside?' the man asked.

'Of course.'

Rose and Bill bent down and entered the hut. It was dark. The hairs on the back of Rose's head stood on end and she felt a strange tingling down her spine. She was standing in the very spot where Captain Gardiner had conversed with Dingarn, through an interpreter, all those many years ago.

She gulped feeling quite dizzy.

'Steady on, old girl,' Bill murmured and put his arm around her. They came out back into the bright sunshine.

'Could I take your photo?' the white man asked.

'Yes, yes that's fine,' Rose said.

The white man with the camera took several and wrote down their address so that he could send copies to them. It turned out that the men worked in a museum in a nearby town where the present king of the Zulus lived.

After an interesting conversation they all returned to their cars and Stephen prepared to drive back to Durban. Rose couldn't thank Stephen and Judith enough. 'It has been a wonderful experience, thank you so much.'

Rose had seen Gardiner Street, the main street, poor little Julia's gravestone, been shown the suburb Berea where Captain Gardiner and his second wife Elizabeth and two surviving children had lived for a short while before the Zulu Wars. Most interestingly and enthrallingly, she had stood where Captain Gardiner had stood talking to the bloodthirsty chieftain. She had come to understand the fear with which South Africans of European descent lived and so she marvelled at the courage Captain Gardiner had shown when he actually lived with Dingarn and his Zulus. Was it the courage of a man who had such faith in God and his son Jesus Christ, or was it the courage of a man who didn't care whether he lived or died? Rose didn't know. With her mission in Durban accomplished Rose and Bill flew to Capetown.

Capetown was a beautiful city dominated by Table Mountain. There were far more white faces in the crowds than there had been in Durban, but the fear was still there. When they booked into their hotel the receptionist told them on no account to go into the square at the back of the hotel because it was too dangerous. 'It's fine during the week when all the stalls are there but don't go there on Saturday or Sunday.'

They went on two bus trips. The first to visit the wineries with their picturesque houses, and the wine was good too. They went down to the southernmost tip of the Cape where there was a lighthouse. Happily walking along the path to the lighthouse, Rose suddenly looked to the sea crashing on rocks hundreds of feet below. Recalling that she suffered from vertigo, she sat down and told Bill could go no further. He walked to the lighthouse while Rose sat huddled, watching with horror as native boys happily skipped down the narrow path. Somehow she struggled back to the bus clutching Bill's arm and not daring to look on either side.

They caught the Blue Train back to Johannesburg from where they would fly back to Australia. The Blue Train was her indulgence; it cost the equivalent of one thousand Australian dollars for the twelve-hour trip. On the rain, they had their personal butler, who, at the ring of their bell, would provide them with any drink or food they desired. There was also a beautiful menu in the dining room, but after it Rose felt she could eat nothing more.

The scenery was beautiful. They went through the Big Karoo and the Little Karoo (or was it the other way round?) and were due to arrive in Johannesburg next morning. As the train grew closer to the city they noticed the armed guards on the stations. Before they arrived it was announced over the public address system that on no account should any of the passengers leave the train and wander around the station. They must stay in their cabins until their designated driver or taxi driver came to collect them. Fear again.

Going straight to their hotel near the airport, they had several hours wait for their flight to Sydney. When Rose asked when their Qantas flight was due to leave she was met with blank looks. They didn't seem to have even heard of Qantas.

Rose felt sick. 'How are we supposed to know when our flight is ready to board?'

'Don't worry, Rose, it'll be okay,' Bill tried to sound reassuring.

They finally did get on the right plane and were both glad to be home again. 'We don't realise how lucky we are,' Rose said in relief. Bill agreed.

By contrast, on their trip to Tierra del Fuego they found it was the journey that proved to be difficult not the destination itself. It did not start well. They had a few hours in Mexico City waiting to catch their flight to Lima in Peru. Rose had developed a migraine. She had begun to develop migraines late in life and had always dreaded getting one when they were travelling. This was the first one she had in all the travelling they had done. The paid was excruciating and the various medications her doctor had prescribed didn't help. She knocked herself out with some tablets but the next day felt tired and giddy.

The group with which they were travelling had a meeting with their tour guide explaining what would happen over the next few days. Their hotel was situated in a safer part of Lima. 'It's okay to visit the shops in the immediate vicinity, but don't wander any further, it's dangerous,' the guide advised them.

Rose and Bill exchanged glances. Here we go again, Rose thought.

Rose had heard many stories about how scary visiting South America could be. There were kidnappings, people just disappeared, and were even murdered. Rose thought they were experienced enough as travellers to cope with any eventualities and it had been her dream for many years to reach Tierra del Fuego where Captain Gardiner had died. There were men with guns guarding banks and official buildings, rather dimming her desire to go shopping.

After Lima they were going to spend a few days in the Amazon Jungle.

After flying over the Andes they landed in Iquitos, where they embarked in a boat travelling down the river to the jungle guest house. As they glided along, watching little boats packed with people's possessions and bigger boats carrying tourists, Rose couldn't believe she was actually on the Amazon River.

The first things they encountered in the jungle were super-sized mosquitoes. Each bed had a mosquito net, but Rose discovered to her horror the next morning that there were holes in hers and she had spent the night with the mosquitoes instead of being protected from them. She sprayed herself with most of the bottle of perfume she had bought in the duty free shop in Sydney to try and ease the itch from dozens of mozzie bites.

They were taken into the jungle to visit a village but the entertainment provided by the natives was so touristy they wondered if any of it was authentic. In the jungle itself the only wild life they saw was the butterflies and ants. It was explained that the animals were nocturnal, so they were taken out in a boat at night by two men who had powerful torches which they shone around the surrounding trees. Rose and her friends couldn't help giggling; they could see no animals.

'Shush, you'll frighten them away,' the men told them.

They dutifully kept quiet. Back on the main river and back to Iquitos where they spent the night before returning the Lima. They were scheduled to fly to Cuzco the next day. It was high in the mountains and flights were often cancelled because of bad weather. They arrived at the airport and were told there were no seat reservations, just first in, best dressed. They waited. There were no seats or benches, so eventually they sat on the concrete floor. They waited. After three hours they were told all flights to Cuzco had been cancelled. Dejectedly they returned to their hotel and went through the same performance the next morning. This time they were lucky and after two hours they were on their way to Cuzco.

Bill had caught influenza when they were staying in the jungle and didn't feel very well. The moment they arrived they were all plied with coca tea which was supposed to combat the effects of altitude sickness. That night Rose began to feel terribly unwell. They were due to do Machu Pichu the next day which was one of the highlights of the trip. Rose had never given altitude sickness a thought, but with her history of headaches and migraines she should have known better. She had also caught Bill's flu and spent the evening and the night vomiting, her head splitting with the most diabolic pain she had ever known. Bill kept plying her with cups of coca tea but to no avail.

What to do? Obviously they couldn't go on to Manchu Pichu which was even higher than Cuzco, so the next morning they were put on a plane back to Lima by their sympathetic tour guide. 'Don't worry, someone will meet you, and in a couple of days I've booked you on a flight direct to Rio. We'll all arrive there a day later. Don't worry,' he kept saying.

Rose knew the cardinal rule for travelling with groups was that you never left your group, and now they were doing just that. She felt too sick to cry and couldn't have been more disappointed. Brave or foolish, foolish or brave - kept going through her mind, but all she felt was foolish.

They landed in Lima and Rose's head stopped hurting. They were taken to the airport for their overnight trip to Rio. When they went through security, they had to leave the cheerful little tour guide. They were alone – alone in the midst of throngs of people queuing to board flights all over South America. Alone, surrounded by crowds of people very few of whom could speak English. Rose panicked. 'How do you know which gate to go to, how do we know which plane to board?'

Don't worry, we'll just ask,' Bill sounded more confident than he felt.

'But nobody will speak English. They won't know what we're talking about.'

'Somebody will,' Bill replied emphatically.

They approached different people in different lines. 'Are you going to Rio?'

They responded with blank stares.

At last someone replied. 'Yes, I'm going to Rio, this is the right gate for the plane to Rio.'

By the time they had settled in to the aircraft Rose started worrying about the visas. Before leaving Australia they had to get visas for Peru, Bolivia, Brazil and Argentina. They had missed Bolivia and were two days early arriving in Brazil. Would their visa be dated with the day they were supposed to arrive - two days hence? Rose felt sick. She couldn't sleep, and not that she ever slept on planes but the night seemed endless.

'Don't worry, it'll be okay.' Bill assured her.

'How do you know? Oh, I wish we'd never left home.'

'Where's my brave Rose then?'

'I'm not brave, I'm just silly....'

On arrival they picked up their luggage and presented themselves to the customs official. He glanced perfunctorily at their passports, stamped them and on they went. 'Thank heavens,' Rose sighed. All that worry for nothing.

Outside there was a lovely little man holding a placard on which was written 'Mr and Mrs Harrison'. She could have kissed him. He drove them to their hotel which was across the street from the famous Copacabana Beach. Rose collapsed on the bed.

'Like a cup of tea?' Bill asked.

'I think I need more than a cup of tea!' Rose said with some feeling.

'It's a bit early for alcohol,' Bill pretended to be disapproving.

'What a ghastly night. I can't imagine how Captain Allen went to all these strange places, by himself, not knowing what was going to happen to him.'

'He was a brave man.'

When she had recovered sufficiently, Rose examined the messages placed on the walls of their room. One said that on no account should they leave any valuables in their room. Never go out wearing jewellery, not even wedding rings, it was best left, with their passports and travel documents, in a safety deposit box provided and stored by the reception clerk. Another message warned of the dangers on the Copacabana Beach: again no valuables and ladies were advised not to take handbags when away from the hotel.

'Well, I'm going to sit on that beach even if it is dangerous,' Rose announced, but they felt uncomfortable and didn't stay long.

Gemstones were next on Rose's list. She had been told they were inexpensive and available in Brazil. They made their way to the nearest jeweller's shop, Rose without her handbag, Bill with some money, their credit cards and travellers cheques in a money belt safely hidden beneath his shirt. In the jewellery shop not one piece of jewellery could be seen.

'May I help you? What are you looking for?' a pleasant lady enquired.

'Well, I really want to see some aquamarines, and some other stones as gifts to my daughter and granddaughters,' Rose replied.

The lady disappeared and returned with a little bag in her hands. 'We have to be very careful,' she explained, 'We've been burgled three times in the last few months. The thieves managed to get in through the roof. Do you see that man who looks like a hobo hanging round the entrance?'

Rose and Bill looked round carefully.

'He is actually an armed guard with a gun in his pocket.'

Suddenly Rose lost interest in buying jewellery although she managed to acquire some aquamarines and gifts for her family.

'You must hide these,' the shop assistant told them. Bill put them in his money belt under his shirt.

'Do be careful,' the lady urged. 'Don't make eye contact with the passers-by. Most of them only want to sell you things and you'll never get rid of them.'

They returned to the hotel as quickly as possible.

'What sort of a place is this?' Rose demanded.

'A very dangerous one.' Bill replied.

They were relieved when the rest of the group arrived. There seemed to be a little more safety in numbers. Their main excursion to Rio was to visit the base of the statue of Jesus that dominated the city. Knowing her tendency to attacks of vertigo when she looked down from great heights, Rose was not looking forward to it. 'I guess I'll just have to close my eyes.'

'I'll tell you what the view looks like,' Bill offered cheerfully.

When they finally arrived at the viewing platform, Rose stood well back from the edge. The view was magnificent. It even gave Sydney Harbour a run for its money.

They were due to visit the Iguassu Falls, but as frequently happens in South America, there was a strike; their direct flight was cancelled and they had to fly to Buenos Aires, wait a couple of hours, then fly back to the falls.

The falls were absolutely magnificent. For miles water tumbled into the river below in a truly natural wonder of the world.

Next day they wearily returned to Buenos Aires with the main purpose of their trip, visiting Tierra del Fuego still to come. They had an introduction to an Anglican Minister living in the city but their meeting with him was most disappointing. He seemed to think visiting Tierra del Fuego was a waste of time. Captain Gardiner's visit to its shores was so long ago he didn't think anyone remembered it anymore. Feeling crushed, Rose wondered why they had bothered to come. They'd missed the trip to Machu Pichu and everywhere seemed so dangerous and frightening, and now their entire reason for it was disappearing before her eyes. She felt great sympathy for her great-great-grandfather who had suffered so much sadness and frustration in his life that her disappointments seemed tiny in comparison. His beautiful wife had died, his beautiful daughter had died, his efforts to bring a better life to the Zulus in South Africa and the natives of South America had met with frustration, failure and finally, his death.

With heavy hearts Rose and Bill and another couple, Owen and Beverly Wright, set out for Ushuiaa, the capital of Argentinian Tierra del Fuego, the land of fire. The rest of the group went to a wine growing district in Argentina. Their flight was nicknamed the 'milk run', as it stopped in every major town from Buenos Aires to Ushuaia. It took six hours. After flying over the Magellan Straits they soon touched down in Ushuiaa.

When they emerged from the plane Rose gasped. The scene in front of her was so beautiful. In the distance were snow-capped mountains, beneath the white was a band of crimson red, a forest of Arctic Beech trees. Beneath the trees was the Beagle Channel which looked like a plate of blue glass. Reaching this destination was only possible by plane or ship, in the winter it could be cut off for weeks at a time. Now it looked incredibly unreal in its beauty. 'It's so beautiful,' Rose declared. 'I had no idea....' She clutched Bill's arm as they walked across the tarmac.

They were met by bubbly and friendly Marie Sol, their tour guide. She bundled the four of them into the waiting car as the air was cold even though the sun was shining. 'I'll take you to your hotel,' she announced, 'Then I thought we'd have a drive round the national park. We've just had a fall of snow and in the autumn the beech trees are beautiful. I take it you had lunch on the plane?'

'Yes, thank you, that sounds a good idea,' Bill replied.

Rose ventured hesitantly. 'I'm actually the great-great-granddaughter of Captain Allen Gardiner. Have you heard of him?'

'Of course,' Marie Sol agreed enthusiastically. 'This visit must be very important to you.'

Rose felt a wave of relief. They did remember him after all. 'We were hoping we could go to the beach where he died.'

'Well, I don't know if that can be arranged, it's pretty hard to get there. I think you'd have to get in touch with the navy,' Marie Sol replied. 'But leave it with me, I'll try and work something out.'

Bill squeezed Rose's hand and smiled. Their trip to the furthest-most end of the earth might not be in vain. The national park was beautiful but it was cold, as cold as midwinter in Armidale. After returning the Whites to the hotel, Marie Sol took Rose and Bill to the local museum. Here they were met by a girl who could speak English and a young man who couldn't. Both seemed absolutely delighted to meet Rose.

'The curator of the museum would like to meet you. He can't speak English but I will interpret for you,' the girl said.

They were led into a comfortable room with a large desk on which were piles of documents. A most distinguished-looking gentleman stood up and waved for them to sit on the chairs provided. As he spoke, the interpreter told them that he welcomed them and that he was deeply honoured and impressed by the visit of one of the great Captain's descendants.

Rose replied that in turn they were honoured to be there, and impressed by the beauty of their surroundings. 'It is one of the most beautiful places I have ever seen!'

The curator beamed at his guests, and there followed a disjointed conversation as both sides spoke through the interpreter. When they stood to leave he shook them both warmly by the hand and told their interpreter that they were to have a tour of the whole museum, especially the rooms upstairs that were not usually shown to visitors. They were fascinated by the exhibits in the museum, especially the wedding gowns worn by the Bridge's family.

The Reverend Bridges had established a mission in Tierra del Fuego some years after Allen Gardiner's death. His family later purchased a large area of land where they established a sheep farm. His descendants still owned some of this land but Rose had received no reply to the letters she had written to them from Australia.

As they were leaving, Carlos told Rose and Bill through the interpreter that he knew of a film that had been made of the memorial set in the rocks above the beach where Captain Gardiner and his shipmates had died. He also explained how difficult it would be for them to make the trip to this beach in the little time available. Rose and Bill returned to their hotel somewhat comforted by the fact that Allen Gardiner had not been entirely forgotten and by the curator's warm welcome which eased Rose's disappointment somewhat.

Their hotel did not serve dinner so the four walked to the hotel next door for their evening meal. As usual no-one spoke a word of English. There was a little waiter just like Manual out of *Fawlty Towers* and Rose asked hopefully, 'crab?' She had eaten crab in Alaska and in San Francisco but Tierra del Fuego had a reputation for serving the most delicate and sweetest tasting crab in the world.

A little later the waiter returned with plates piled high and several little pots of different sauces. Rose was really enjoying the meal when the thought struck her: Why hadn't Allen and his men been able to catch crab or fish of any kind to save them from starving to death? She couldn't eat another mouthful. Feeling totally overcome, she murmured, 'I don't feel well, I think I'll go back to our hotel.'

Bill gave her a startled look and nodded. She excused herself to the Whites, and on her return to her hotel room lay on the bed with tears streaming down her cheeks. Suddenly the phone rang. She sat up in fright. Who could be ringing? It must be a mistake, nobody knew they were there. She said 'hello' hesitantly.

It was Carlos, the young man from the museum, who somehow even with his lack of English, managed to explain he had found the film of Allen's memorial and would they come around to see it?

'Mañana?' Rose said, using one of the few Spanish words that she knew.

'No, no, no. Now.'

She rushed back to the hotel where Bill was still enjoying his dinner. In only a few minutes, Carlos arrived to drive them to his home. It was a small house with a combined kitchen-living room and upstairs there were obviously bedrooms, and it was in – Gardiner Street! The room was full of happy, laughing people, who made them very welcome. There were four or five women who made endless cups of strong, black coffee. While the film was being setting up, there were children everywhere.

Unaware that Rose and Bill couldn't understand a word they were saying, they came and sat on their knees and showed them their pets, in particular a little turtle. They were all so kind and friendly that Rose immediately felt enveloped in their warmth and love. The men had difficulty with the film. It kept breaking, so they all drank more coffee. One of the women put on her coat.

She must be leaving, Rose thought. 'Adios?' the only other word she knew in Spanish.

The woman shook her head vehemently. A short time later she returned with another woman who turned out to be a school teacher who could speak a little English. At last they could communicate. The men finally fixed the film, and they were able to see footage of beach where Allen Gardiner and his men had died and of the memorial in the rocks above it. When it was finished the school teacher said to Rose and Bill, 'Carlos is going to speak to God.'

They all bowed their heads, even the children were quiet. 'Would you tell them I now wish to speak to God?' Rose started bravely. 'Our Father, who art in heaven hallowed be thy name, thy kingdom come thy will be done, on earth as it is in heaven. Give us this day, our daily bread…' Her mind went totally blank. After a moment she said 'Amen,' and sat down. Bill gave her a startled look. How could she forget the Lord's Prayer? But she had; thank goodness no-one else there would know.

The school teacher asked if they could come and visit them again. Rose shook her head sadly, 'Australia is a long way from here.'

It was getting late and it was time to go. With kisses and hugs all round they said goodbye and piled into Carlos's car with all the children. After fond farewells Rose and Bill wearily made their way back to their room. 'What a wonderful evening!' Rose exclaimed.

Bill agreed. 'Made it all worthwhile.'

'It certainly did.'

Bill was soon in bed and asleep. Rose sat looking out the window at Ushuia. She could see the mission suburb where Reverend Bridges had made his first settlement. If her great-great-grandfather's endeavours had led to the wonderful people they had just met it must have been worthwhile. She thought he had perhaps just wanted someone to come here, how beautiful it was, and not the scary and forbidding 'end of the earth' that she had imagined. She felt his presence as she sat gazing into the darkness.

There was such a feeling of peace and love in the room, as there had been in the humble little cottage that they had visited. She knew he hadn't been afraid when he and his six friends faced death on that lonely beach. He had died peacefully, full of love for his God.

IV

Chapter 8

Mel sat lazily warming herself in the sun. Her eyes squinted as she gazed at the hills in the distance. 'Mel, where are you?' Her mother's voice floated on the balmy air, coming from the house behind her.

'I'm here,' she replied.

'Mel, where are you?' Her mother again.

'I'm here,' she repeated, getting slightly exasperated. 'Oh bother,' she said to herself. 'I suppose I'd better go and see what she wants.'

She took a last look at the scene in front of her: green, rolling hills, gum trees, a few sheep nonchalantly chewing the grass, cattle a bit further away. 'On a clear day you can see to Queensland,' people said. How could they possibly know? Mel asked herself.

Their property stretched about six miles to the north, then dropped a couple of thousand feet into gulf country. Further away the blue hills became hazy. How could anyone possibly know if you could see to Queensland? 'The silly things people say,' she muttered.

'Coming, Mum!' She raised her voice a little, and then slowly disentangled herself from the rock on which she had been sitting. Even on such a sunny day there was still a chill wind. Autumn in New England was perfect, Mel thought. She made her way to the kitchen where she found her mother, Catherine, ferociously stabbing metal skewers into the naked bottom of a chicken. 'Could you give me a hand Mel and do the vegies?' her mother asked. 'I'm running a bit late.'

'You're not running late,' Mel said evenly. 'Besides, it's only for the three of us.' Catherine looked irritated. 'Mel, you know I like to be on time.'

'Yes, Mum,' her daughter replied, deadpan. The fact was her mother not only liked to be on time, she liked to be early. Mel thought of all the functions and outings and the like, where they had invariably been early, arriving long before anyone else.

'Well, I'm a Virgo,' Catherine would say as if that explained all her idiosyncrasies. Mel's father, Stuart, was much more laid-back, but for the sake of peace, he and Mel tried to keep to Catherine's schedule. Mel commenced peeling potatoes, wondering why her usually calm and collected mother seemed so out of sorts even if she was preparing a special dinner because Mel was going back to the university the next day.

The Harrisons killed their own meat, so they had lamb all summer and beef all winter. It was for special occasions that Catherine cooked a baked chicken dinner with stuffing, bread sauce and all the trimmings. She was famous for her baked dinners and she had cooked them so often she always said she could do it with one hand tied behind her back. It was for this reason Mel was worried about her mother; she just didn't seem to be her usual unflustered self.

That night after the dinner, while Catherine was tidying up the kitchen, Mel mentioned this to her father. 'Mum doesn't seem herself lately,' she said. 'Is anything wrong?'

Stuart stumbled away, mumbling something about her 'moods'. Of course, Mel thought. Menopause, why didn't I think of that? 'Has she seen a doctor, Dad?'

'Well, no, but I've been trying to persuade her.'

'She must. Women don't have to suffer these days.'

It could explain her mother's recent behaviour, the irrational, worst thing being that her mother had suddenly taken a violent dislike to Mel's boyfriend Alex. When she had first started to bring him home, Catherine seemed to like him very much. Now she couldn't stand him and didn't try to hide it.

'But Mum, you liked Alex when you first met him,' Mel challenged her mother. 'What has he done to upset you?'

'Nothing, I just don't trust him,' was the short reply.

Mel and Alex made a striking couple. He was tall with dark, wavy hair, an aquiline nose, melting brown eyes and olive skin. A complete contrast to Mel's fair skin, auburn hair and green eyes.

'Cat's eyes, cat's eyes,' the girls at school used to tease her. She had inherited the glorious red hair that appeared so often in women in her family tree. 'It's skipped a generation,' her mother would explain cheerfully when friends asked her if she had known the delivery man, as neither Catherine nor her brother had red hair. Catherine's hair had been blonde as a child but it had shaded to mousy-brown as she got older

Mel had spent her childhood being reminded by her mother to wear hats, long-sleeved blouses and blockout cream. She had been impatient when she was young, annoyed she couldn't sit on the beach and sunbake with her friends. Now she was glad her mother had been so strict and pleased that she didn't have sun-damaged skin.

She had been going out with Alex Douglas for about six months, and thought he was wonderful – kind, funny, and intelligent. At first her mother had agreed with her, but now, strangely, she had completely altered her opinion.

Mel sighed; everything had been so perfect. She was a second-year Agriculture Economics student, and he a third-year accountancy student. He came from Tenterfield, where his father was a stock and station agent. He was a few years older than Mel, as he had gone into his father's business when he left school. Then he and his family had agreed a university degree would be in his best interest. He still wanted to come back and work in his father's business but a few years away from his family appealed to him. He had a younger brother who went to The Armidale School, the prestigious boys' school.

Armidale was an hour's drive south-west from the Harrison's property, but Mel knew Armidale well. She had been to boarding school there, and it was the closest city to her parent's property. Their accountant and lawyer were there and their stock and station agent was also there, and her grandmother Rose. Catherine bought her groceries there.

They did not need to buy fruit and vegetables as Stuart was an ardent grower of anything to eat. They had an orchard with peaches, nectarines, plums, apples, and apricots. They were stewed and put into the freezer when they were in season. Catherine patiently bottled the excess to eat in the winter. She made homemade ice-cream, with cream and condensed milk. Stuart milked the cow every morning. The vegetables he picked half-an-hour before Catherine cooked them, and she also made pickles, relish and chutney from tomatoes, apricots and plums. The shelves of the pantry were always lined with pretty bottles of jam and relish, neatly packed peaches, plums cooked in the Vacola bottling outfit. Mel remembered stirring the darkened juice from bottled plums into the homemade ice-cream.

As Stuart often took out a packed lunch, every week Catherine had a baking day, usually Thursday. She would make biscuits, a slice, a buttered loaf and a cake every week. Their property was long and narrow, facing south to north, and they lived in the southern corner of it. They had built their house on the top of a hill facing north, hopeful of seeing the distant hills and Queensland. There was a large dam to the east of the house, and more hills stood guardian to the south. Their choice of position for the home had not gone down well with Stuart's parents who lived out of sight round the hills.

'You can't live on a view you know,' his mother Lily told Catherine primly.

'I don't intend to live on it,' was Catherine's spirited reply, 'but it will be nice to look at it.'

•

After Mel was born, she and her parents lived in the house Johnny Harrison had built for he and his wife Mary not long after Rose and Bill Harrison had built their house round the other side of the hill. At the time their home was being built, Rose had been upset that Bill's father told him to cut out a room and make the living area smaller. Indeed, Johnny's house was bigger and better than Bill and Rose's, but it was on the wrong side of the hill and didn't have the beautiful view to the north.

When Rose and Bill had chosen the place they wanted to build Mary had looked at Rose coldly. 'You can't live on a view,' she said, 'and you do realise your house will be close to the spot where Bill's Aunt Demelza died?'

'Yes, I knew that,' Rose said gently, 'and every time I look down the hill I'll remember how beautiful and sweet Demelza was.'

Mary gave her a frosty look.

'I know my father's hard to get on with,' Bill explained to Rose. 'He didn't really get over his sister's and his mother's death, and then he went and fought in the trenches in France in the Great War.' As Bill explained, his father Johnny had fallen in love with a French nurse towards the end of the war. He had received a burst of shrapnel in his leg and spent several weeks in hospital recovering from his wounds. The French girl returned his feelings but as she wouldn't leave France and he was determined not to stay there a minute longer than he had to, he returned to Glenfoyle, where he was more morose and introverted than when he had left. Jack decided to move to Armidale where his sisters and their families were brighter company than his son. 'You must find yourself a wife,' he suggested to Johnny.

It was, however, a few more couple years before Johnny married Mary. She was the youngest of four sisters and was in her late-thirties when they married. She came from a pioneering family so knew all about country life.

'I know.' Rose said. 'I do try and understand but Mary's so cold and unfriendly too.'

Bill agreed that his mother was a cold person, lacking emotion.

Luckily for Rose, Bill took after his grandfather, Jack. Jack with the bright blue eyes, a cheerful disposition and warm and affectionate.

'Of course if he'd been like his father I would never have married him,' Rose told herself ruefully, and knew she would never be accepted by his parents because she wasn't a 'country girl.'

•

There was only one drawback to the first few years of Stuart and Catherine's marriage, and that was the fact that she had no luck having babies. After several miscarriages, Catherine was heartbroken. She would lose the baby in the first few weeks of pregnancy, so when she became pregnant for the fourth time her doctor told her sternly: 'You must stay in bed for nine months.'

'Stay in bed! I can't do that.'

The doctor said gently, 'If you want to have a baby you must.' Catherine's eyes filled with tears, her lips quivered. 'But who'll look after Stuart?'

'He's a grown man quite capable of looking after himself,' he said gently; 'I'm sure your mother would love to come and take care of you all.'

Catherine was ecstatic when the beautiful bundle of joy that was Melanie Jane, came into the world.

'She's just so beautiful,' she murmured to Stuart secretly. She was delighted the baby was a girl and Stuart seemed to be just as delighted.

Catherine's mother Poppy felt her heart jump when she saw the little girl with tufts of red hair just the same colour as her own. 'I think Catherine was meant to have a daughter,' she told her husband. For some reason, she thought that the lost little babies had been little boys.

Johnny and Mary had moved to town and died within a few years of each other before Mel was born. Mel grew up to adore her father's parents, Granny Rose and Granddad Bill as she called them. She was always enthralled by Rose's stories of her family, the Gardiners, and her famous ancestor Captain Allen Gardiner.

Her mother, Catherine, came from Tamworth where her father was a doctor. She had gone to school at New England Girls' School in Armidale, and had met Stuart when he was a school boy at The Armidale School.

Rose would go out to Glenfoyle from time to time to check on the building of Stuart and Catherine's house. When she did so, she would wander down the hill and sit on the spot where she had been told Demelza had died.

'I think Demelza was happy when she died,' she told Bill one night.

'What makes you think that?' Bill said.

'Because I don't get bad vibes when I sit there, I get happy ones. It was a lovely sunny day, she was riding down the paddock with her father and brother and the boy next door – I think she had a thing for the boy next door. She looked at him and they smiled, and that's when her horse bucked and she fell.'

'When on earth did you dream all that up?' Bill asked sarcastically.

'I didn't dream it up, I felt it,' Rose snapped.

'Good for you, you have a wonderful imagination.'

Rose groaned. 'And men have none at all.'

When Mel was still quite small and Rose lived in the house with the view, she noticed Mel would wander out of the garden and go and sit in the spot that Rose herself had been drawn to.

'Darling,' she asked her granddaughter, 'why do you go and sit in the paddock? There are plenty of pretty places to sit in the garden.'

'I don't know Granny Rose, I just like it there.'

'You like the view of the hills and the paddocks?'

'Yes, but it just feels comfy there. Is it all right for me to go out of the garden?'

'Yes of course, but don't go any further away, will you?'

'No, I'll just stay there.'

Rose told Catherine and begged her not to let the child know it was the place where Demelza had died. 'And make sure Stuart doesn't tell her either.'

'Of course, we'll never mention it, and if she asks why Demelza died, we'll just say she had pneumonia, something like that.'

As Mel grew older she didn't go and sit in the spot as often. Sometimes she would say to her mother, 'I'm just going to sit in my happy place for a while.'

Mel was eight when Granddad Bill died. He had been gradually handing over the running of Glenfoyle to Stuart. He enjoyed overseas trips, especially the ones to Durban and Terra del Fuego. He took great pleasure in pottering round the garden, looking after the many and varied camellias and rhododendrons Rose had planted over the years. Although he had smoked a pipe all his life, he was not plagued by coughs and colds and never had a stomach upset in his life. He had done hard physical work since he was a boy, and was not one to sit around watching television.

One Saturday morning he seemed off-colour and Rose rang Stuart to tell him she was taking his father in to see the doctor.

'Do you want me to come with you?' Stuart asked.

'No, I don't think so. I don't think it's anything to worry about, he just doesn't seem to be himself.'

'Let me know if you need me.'

'Thank you dear, I'll be in touch.'

The doctor seemed as mystified as Rose. Bill had never had high blood pressure but now it was lower than normal although really nothing to worry about, so the doctor said. 'How about we put him into hospital for the night and we'll do some more tests tomorrow.'

By morning Bill's condition was deteriorating. The doctor suggested Rose send for her children.

This can't be happening, Bill's never sick, she thought. Stuart, Catherine and Mel arrived in an hour and sat with Rose while the medical staff did more tests.

'What is wrong with Dad?' Stuart asked.

'They don't seem to know,' his mother replied. 'I hope the girls can get here soon.'

Bill's sister Louise arrived that night but his other sister, Jane was unable to get there until the following morning.

Rose, Stuart and Louise were at the hospital early next morning. Bill seemed comfortable and not in pain, but before Jane arrived they noticed doctors and nurses rushing to Bill's room.

Rose clung to Stuart. 'I can't believe it, I can't believe it,' she said. 'He's never been sick a day in his life.'

In a few minutes the grave-faced doctor appeared. 'I'm sorry, Rose, but Bill has had a heart attack and – we couldn't save him.'

Rose gave a little moan as she clung to Stuart, Catherine and Louise.

When Jane arrived she was upset that she had not been able to say goodbye to her father. 'None of us did, Sis,' Stuart said comfortably. 'It happened so quickly none of us did.'

It was some months before Rose recovered sufficiently from her husband's sudden death to make plans for the future.

'I have decided to move to town. I'm going to live in Armidale,' she told Stuart, Catherine and Mel as they sat having morning tea.

'You're sure, Mum? You're quite sure?' Stuart sounded surprised.

'Yes, quite sure, I'll find a nice little house – not too little, I'll need enough room for all my family to come and stay,'

'But won't you miss this house that you and Granddad built, and your garden, and your camellias – and us?' Catherine added jokingly.

'Of course I will, but I can always come and visit and you can pop in when you come to town.' 'Besides,' she added, 'I never was a country girl.'

They all laughed. Mel went and put her arms round her grandmother's neck. 'I'll miss you Granny Rose,' and tears came to the little girl's eyes.

'I'll miss you too,' Rose was getting a bit weepy too, 'but we'll still see a lot of each other. I'll come out for birthdays and Christmas and when the camellias are flowering.'

They eventually found a pleasant house in Faulkner Street on the south side of the town. It was elevated enough to escape the worst frosts and the smog, and there were enough bedrooms for when family came to stay.

'Of course I'll have to have the house repainted. It's all cream and beige, I can't stand it,' she said emphatically.

'That means a new carpet as well,' Catherine twinkled.

'Of course.'

Rose started sorting her things, a long and painful task. They fell into three categories, things she loved and couldn't live without, furniture her son and two daughters might like to have, and things that had to go to the rubbish tip.

Finally all was ready for her to leave. The house in Armidale had been painted pretty blues and mauves, the outside pale grey and dark grey and there was a new blue carpet.

'Feel free to decorate as much as you want to,' Rose told Catherine. 'You won't upset my feelings, I'm just glad you'll have the house with the view. It's lovely sitting out the front on a sunny morning and looking at the rows and rows of hills.'

'All the way to Queensland!'

The two women laughed. It had become a family joke, after all who could tell if you could see Queensland or not?

Finally Rose went through the documents in her husband's desk. She had been dreading the thought of doing it as it would bring back so many memories. She must do it so she armed herself with a brandy and set to work.

At the back of one of the cubby holes was a little packet of very old and faded letters that Rose was sure she had never seen before.

Very gently and carefully, Rose unwrapped them and found to her astonishment they were letters written by her great-great-grandfather Allen Gardiner to Bill's great-great-grandfather John Gregory, his neighbour and best friend.

The tears streamed down Rose's cheeks and her fingers trembled as she read the precious words.

'I can't believe it,' she thought. Precious moments from the past. Suddenly brought to life in the present. Almost as if Allen Gardiner and John Gregory were there in the room with her. She took a gulp of brandy. What a wonderful way for the friendship of these two outstanding men to be brought back to life through the letters. How extraordinary that she Rose, a Gardiner, had married Bill the descendant of Allen's best friend John Gregory.

They had kept in touch with Bill's Gregory relations at Maitland and frequently called on them on their way to or from the wool sales at Newcastle. The side of the family had prospered in the hundred years since Adam had bought Milly's block. They had planted grape vines and had slowly developed the whole property into a vineyard. They called the chardonnay they produced 'Melrose Park' and it had become well-known around Australia and overseas. The Harrisons had prospered as well, of course, After buying the McDougall property, they had bought more sheep, and with the income from wool boom after the Second World War they had increased their cattle numbers, changing from Hereford to Santa Gertrudis.

Rose realised she must get hold of Stuart and find out if he knew anything about the letters she had found. She left a message with Catherine asking Stuart to come around that evening. When Rose showed him the faded bundle of letters he shook his head. 'No, I've never seen them before.'

Rose was still a little shaken with the excitement of finding a link between the two families, the Gardiners and the Gregorys.

'This really means a great deal to you doesn't it?' Stuart asked.

'Yes it does. I think perhaps your father had never even looked at them. I'm so glad I found them before I left here.' Her voice started to get a bit wobbly.

'Come on Mum, let's celebrate.' He sniffed Rose's glass. 'What have you been drinking? Brandy? Mum I'm surprised at you.'

'Oh, that was hours ago.'

'Well, I'll pour you another one. I take it you have still a little whisky somewhere?'

They clinked glasses. 'To the Gardiners.' 'And to the Gregorys.'

Rose soon settled down to life in Armidale. She pretended she wasn't nervous living alone, and after a few months found that she wasn't anymore.

She joined the University of the Third Age group and went to lectures on local history, philosophy and music appreciation. She enjoyed having coffee in town with friends and still had lunch parties although the numbers shrank over the years. Sadly most of her friends were now widows, but being women they were quite capable of looking after themselves.

Stuart was surprised his mother hadn't immediately filled her garden with camellias and rhododendrons as she loved them so much.

'No dear,' she said firmly. 'In the first place the soil isn't right. It's alkaline not acid, and then the climate doesn't suit them. The frosts are too severe in the winter and it's too hot in the summer. I'll just come out and enjoy the garden at Glenfoyle,' Rose went on cheerfully. 'Anyway, my bones are getting a bit old for gardening.'

'Rubbish,' Stuart disagreed with his mother. 'You're as fit as a spring chicken.'

Rose laughed. 'I think not.'

Chapter 9

Mel packed her things into an overnight bag, pulled her hair into a ponytail and filled her car with petrol. She went back into the house to say goodbye to her mother. They hugged. Lectures started again the next day so Mel was returning to Armidale.

'Take care,' Catherine called, as she watched her daughter drive away in her little yellow Honda. It had been a present from her father on Mel's eighteenth birthday.

Mel set off along the gravel road which stretched two miles from home to the Guyra-Ebor Road. She drove past her grandparent's house and the derelict garden which had once surrounded her great-grandparents home. All that remained of this once loved garden was a big old magnolia tree. Mel felt a slight shiver down her spine as she saw the magnolia tree. For some reason the sight of it had always troubled her. She did not know why. Perhaps because it was the only thing left in the once loved garden. Lonely and forlorn it stood sentinel to the past. From the stories her parents told her there was something strange and something sad about the old magnolia tree.

Mel drove on, her spirits lifting as she turned to the right on the bitumen road, and she was now facing west in the direction of Guyra.

For ten miles she drove along before turning to the left on the Rockvale Road, gravel again, a winding road often sprinkled with kangaroos that came to get the green pickings by the side of the road. In the autumn of 2010, there had been drought for nearly ten years in most parts of New South Wales. Some parts were worse than others, especially west of Armidale and Guyra. Where Me's family lived there had been rain from time to time and some good seasons but people were wondering if the drought would ever end.

Mel crossed a couple of creeks. In wet times they could become impassable and to get home from Armidale she would have to detour through Guyra. There was only a trickle of water in them now, one was quite dry.

Mel was looking forward to seeing her friends again, Emma, Tony, and Tina, her flatmate. They all went to university in Armidale. And, of course, there would be Alex. Her heart skipped a beat at the thought of seeing him again.

Mel's mind wandered back to the day her parents had taken her in to Armidale to New England Girls' School for her first day there as a boarder in year seven. Before going to NEGS, she had attended Wongwibinda, the little primary school about five miles to the east of her home, along the Ebor Road. It was a one-teacher school with only a few pupils, but over the years, her grandfather, her father and her aunts had all attended Wongwibinda for primary schooling.

In his time, her grandfather had ridden a horse to school; later her father and aunts and some of the neighbour's children all piled into the family station wagon driven by his mother, who patiently took the children to school and brought them home again for about fourteen years. At the time that there was an antimony mine on the edge of the Harrison's property, the number of pupils at the school had swelled dramatically – over thirty children from kindergarten to year six had been taught by one teacher. The teacher had a residence, a librarian, and help from the pupils. One such teacher was so overcome by his noisy and uncontrollable pupils, he only lasted three days before asking for a transfer. By the time it was Mel's turn to go to Wongwibinda school Wongwibinda there were only fifteen children in attendance.

While Mel was at primary school, Catherine, Stuart, and Mel would go to the Sawtell for their annual holiday. A relatively quiet, seaside town, Sawtell was only a two hour drive from home. Half-an-hour to Ebor (famous many years before as the site of the beer-with-no-pub in contradiction of Slim Dusty's popular song), half-an-hour to Dorrigo, then down treacherous Dorrigo Mountain. Bad weather could block this way to the coast, at times there could be rock falls or little waterfalls cut this winding but scenically beautiful road:

Once down the hill they drove through Bellingen then on to Sawtell. Here Stuart indulged his love of fishing, and Catherine and Mel swam at the beach and paddled through the rock pools, looking for sea creatures. Mel had to wear big floppy hats, big dark glasses, long-sleeved shirts and jeans. She sometimes wondered that her mother had let her wear a bathing suit to go surfing – well covered with sunscreen of course.

After primary school, going to NEGS as a boarder was a shock to the system for Mel. When Mel's grandmother, Lily, had gone to the school in the late 1940s it had only taken boarders. Now girls came from Queensland, from families on the land in the west and north of NSW, and came from Sydney. To help in compete with the now-academically respectable Presbyterian Ladies College, NEGS had introduced a riding school, so that country girls could bring their horses to school. Mel's father had given away horses and did most of his mustering and stock work with motorbikes. Although Mel could ride she wasn't a 'horsey' person and didn't want to do the riding course at NEGS.

Shortly after she arrived there, Mel recovered from the shock of being surrounded by hundreds of girls and many teachers and started to make friends. Some of the girls in her class she knew slightly. One of these was Emma Maxwell, whose parents lived west of Bundarra. They hit it off straight away. Emma was a plump little blonde with an infectious giggle.

Emma's family property was caught in the drought. Their land seemed to be in a rain shadow and when there was rain about they didn't get any. Nonetheless, Emma's parents were determined their children would have a good education. Emma's brother, Brian, went to The Armidale School while she attended New England Girls' School.

During those first few weeks of miserable homesickness, Emma would be often by Mel's side, chattering about nothing in particular, making her laugh in spite of herself. Mel felt stressed by so many girls she didn't know, teachers she didn't know, and longed for the wide open spaces and rolling hills of home. She longed for her own bedroom, her cat Twinkle, her father's quiet support, and most of all, she longed for the gentle, kindly unconditional love of her mother.

At home Catherine's heart too was aching for her daughter but she knew that leaving home and meeting new problems was vital to her daughter's development.

As the weeks went by Mel realised how much she was learning from her teachers, and how she was learning to relate to other girls. Over time, the house-mistress didn't seem so cold and unfriendly as she had first thought she was.

Mel and Emma sat side-by-side in the class room and so they got into occasional trouble by whispering to each other when they were supposed to be studying. They both liked swimming and tennis, although with

Mel's fair skin she had to use blockout cream, something Emma had make sure she kept applying it.

'You're as bad as my mother,' Mel complained. 'She's always nagging me to slap on the block out to cover up from the sun.'

'And so you should!' Emma stated. 'You don't want to spoil your beautiful fair skin. You don't know how lucky you are. In a few years the boys will be lining up to take you out.'

'What rubbish!' Mel answered. 'I'm the Ugly Duckling. I'm not pretty like you.'

'You mark my words,' Emma announced, 'In a few years you will be the most beautiful girl at NEGS.'

Mel threw a book at her friend. 'And pigs might fly!'

After what seemed an eternity, they were allowed to see their parents and then, joy of joy, to have a weekend at home. The pattern was set and life at school settled down to routine.

The years went by too quickly and Mel did change from the ugly duckling into the beautiful swan. Emma was just as popular with the boys. Her bright personality and quick wit made it easy for her to make friends inside and outside school. Moreover, Emma and Mel felt they had each found the sister that nature had not given them.

Once she went to NEGS, holidays at Sawtell lost their charm for Mel. Most of her friends went to Yamba for their beach holidays. Yamba was further north along the coast than Sawtell and so further from home. The trip now required them to drive through Tyringham, then to the outskirts of Grafton, and on to the coast. It was not possible to go to Yamba with a view to escaping Armidale, because many Armidelians had the same idea. It was a popular place for New England dwellers in general, and the teenagers all wanted to see their friends there. There were drink-parties for the oldies and teenage parties fraught with the possibility of gate-crashers or under-age daughters being plied with alcohol.

The latter prospect decided Catherine and Stuart to take Mel to a different part of Australia. For them, this meant missing Yamba in January which didn't please their daughter. 'You're just being spoil sports,' Mel complained.

'Don't be silly, we are going to take you to Darwin, Broome, and Perth. Much more exciting than Yamba.'

Mel pouted. 'But we're not going till the winter. We could go to Yamba too.'

'No, we couldn't,' Catherine said firmly.

They flew to Brisbane, which Mel still found hot and sticky even in the middle of winter. From Brisbane they flew to Darwin, a city that was virtually destroyed by a cyclone on Christmas Day 1974. As a result, the buildings all looked smart and new, but although it was September, it was still hot and sticky. In northern Australia, there are no seasons as such, just the wet and the dry. The atmosphere was tropical and casual. To Mel it seemed like a different country from her home four-thousand feet above sea level in the New England tablelands with its cold winters, frost, and occasional snow falls.

'I can't say I'd like to live here. It's too hot,' she told her parents.

Catherine agreed; her daughter's fair colouring did not suit a tropical climate. They then flew to Broome on the coast of Western Australia, famous for pearls and tourists. They flew over the Bungle Bungles, extraordinary hills weathered by millions of years of sun and rain. They stayed at a beautiful resort close to the famous Cable Beach. There were half a dozen restaurants, three or four swimming pools, a shop, and very comfortable accommodation. Stuart wanted to go fishing, Catherine wanted to go pearl shopping, and Mel enjoyed just being there.

It was strange seeing the sun setting into the sea to the west when she was used to seeing it rise from the sea on the eastern coast.

They strolled across and sat on the sand of Cable Beach. 'I thought there are supposed to be camels on the beach,' Mel exclaimed.

'Look behind you,' her mother said quietly.

A quick look made Mel start with fright. Three camels stood only a few yards away. 'Like a ride?' the young man with them cheerfully offered.

'No, thank you,' Mel stammered. He laughed, and moved on.

The next day Stuart set off early for a day's fishing and Catherine and Mel took a bus into the town to do some serious pearl shopping. Catherine loved pretty things – jewellery, clothes, flowers and shopping for pearls brought a gleam to her eyes. After visiting three or four pearl shops and, to Mel's embarrassment by looking at almost everything they had to offer, Catherine bought a pair of pale pink earrings set with tiny pink Argyle diamonds. She bought Mel a necklace of baroque pearls which Mel knew she would always treasure.

They went on a trip to beaches north of Broome where the sand was a dramatic orange red. Then they went on a very long bus trip through the Kimberley, passing through Fitzroy crossing. The scenery was disappointingly flat and boring, with only the anthills and the bulging trunks of the boab trees to break the monotony. At their destination, the Beeke Gorge, they clambered into a little boat and went downstream for a few miles. There were a few crocodiles along the bank, yet Mel was not overly impressed by the fourteen-hour trip.

Arriving home on a cold windy day Mel was oh, so glad at the cool weather and couldn't wait to ring Emma and tell her all about her travels.

When Mel had finished her higher school certificate examinations which signalled the end of her sixth and final year at NEGS, Catherine and Stuart decided to take her to New Zealand instead of letting her go to the infamous 'schoolies week' at the Gold Coast. This was claimed – by those taking part – as a rite-of-passage to adulthood but was often just an excuse to indulge in alcohol, drugs and unruly behaviour.

Mel thought it was a strange coincidence that his particular week her parents offered to take her to New Zealand. She argued the point but she was not really tempted by alcohol, drugs or wild behaviour; she was a little bit prim and proper and she didn't like feeling out of control. Basically she was a little shy and felt uncomfortable with people she did not know very well. While Emma could chat away to anyone and everyone, Mel would seem aloof and was quiet because she didn't want to say or do the wrong thing. Her parents were loving and kind but, being an only child, she never had the rough and tumble of brothers and sisters. She kept her thoughts to herself and seemed quietly self-assured. At times her mother knew Mel was wrestling with some inner problem and did her best to coax her out of her shell. As any mother does, she worried what the future might hold for her beautiful, sensitive daughter.

Granny Rose was thrilled the family had decided to go to New Zealand. She told Stuart the best fishing spots and gave Catherine the phone numbers of all the relatives to contact.

As they flew over the Tasman Sea on the way from Brisbane to Auckland there was excitement in Catherine and Mel's faces. Stuart was delighted to see his wife and daughter look so animated and happy.

For his part, Stuart was also looking forward to this holiday. He was the sort of man who worked hard and worried hard and over the last few years there had been plenty of both. Unreliable weather and unreliable prices for wool, lambs and cattle, plus all the new rates and regulations made life on the land more and more difficult. Things had changed so much since his grandfather had run the property over fifty years ago.

In those days he had not bred his own sheep but bought wethers from far western New South Wales. They were brought to the tablelands by drovers often taking months to complete the long trip. Then in 1950 he bought ewes and rams and started developing his own fine wool merino sheep. This created a lot more work due to lambing and the need to ensure that shearing was over before the ewes had their lambs. Another change was moving from Hereford cattle, which because of their white faces were prone to eye cancer and in a lush season they died from bloat. By purchasing Santa Gertrudis bulls and joining them with Hereford cows Stuart gradually got rid of the white faces on his cattle and with more dry seasons than wet, bloat was also a thing of the past.

After the Second World War there was a wool boom and wool growers had more money than they could have dreamt of ever gaining from wool. This income was mostly ploughed back into fences, tractors and improvements to the land, not necessarily to their personal life-styles.

The next change occurred when wool prices went into a decline and fat lambs seemed to be the way to go. Border Leicestershire rams sired Merino-cross lambs and for some years these kept the farm finances in the black. With successive governments, more and more regulations made life more difficult for the people in the bush. There was so much more bookwork with the introduction of the GST and rates regarding clearing country to grow pastures, and Health and Safety laws.

Over the years, dingoes coming in from the gulf country were a problem. Dingo drives were replaced by aerial baiting which kept the wild dogs in check for some years.

'Stuart, what do you think?'

At the sound of his wife's voice he came abruptly back to reality. 'Think? Think about what?'

'Stuart, you haven't heard a word I said,' Catherine said.

'I'm sorry, I was miles away,' Stuart said.

'We're on holiday!' Catherine complained. 'You can just stop thinking about the place for five minutes,' she surmised.

They were going to arrive in Auckland and there stay with Catherine's cousins, Ross and Sally. Then they hired a car and drove to Taupo so that Stuart could have a couple of days fishing, then on to Wellington.

Mel was entranced by the beauty of Lake Taupo, with its three snow-capped mountains, Ruapehu and Tongariro, standing sentinel in the distance. Stuart was not so entranced by the fishing. He waded over knee-deep in the cool waters of the Wahatanni River before it entered the lake, but the trout were too clever and evaded capture.

In Wellington they climbed some steep hills in the suburb of Khandallah where Catherine's aunt and uncle lived. The view of the harbour from the deck of the house was magnificent but Mel realised why it was called 'windy' Wellington. 'Does the wind ever stop blowing?' she asked.

'Not very often,' was the reply.

'Wait 'till you see the South Island.' Catherine was eager for her daughter to see where she had been born. On the short flight from Wellington to Nelson, Catherine couldn't hide her excitement.

A pretty little town, Nelson snuggled between the sea and the mountains which surrounded it to the south. Mel was shown the house in Ronaki Terrace where her grandmother had lived, and the Girls' College where she'd gone to school. They stayed at the Honest Lawyer, a lovely little hotel around the port, and passed the beach where Catherine swam as a child. They had dinner at the Boat Shed restaurant, which had originally of course been a boat shed. It served wonderful seafood meals and was always packed to capacity.

They drove to the wine-making Marlborough District which was an easy drive from Nelson. Lunch was a must at Havelock Mussel Boys. They served mussels in a variety of ways, as they were right on the edge of Queen Charlotte Sound.

Staying in a Bed & Breakfast in one of the many wineries, Catherine and Mel enjoyed wine-tasting and food-tasting while Stuart went fishing. They decided they had the best of the bargain as the trout Stuart continued to evade capture. After a couple of days they flew on to Christchurch and then to Queenstown.

'Rose always said it's the most beautiful place in the whole world,' Catherine enthused as the plane came into land at Queenstown airport. Stuart and Mel exchanged smiles. They too were used to Rose's pride in the country of her birth. She would often say when there were problems and things went wrong: 'Well, I'm going back to New Zealand to live!'

Stuart would laugh and say, 'Can I help you pack?' knowing she would never leave him and his sunburnt country.

As they drove into the town Mel could see why her mother thought it was so beautiful. Lake Wakapito shimmered in the afternoon sun. There was fresh snow on the Remarkables, the mountains behind the lake. It was breathtaking.

'Oh Mum, it is so beautiful,' Mel whispered. Catherine squeezed her daughter's hand, her eyes filling with tears. Stuart looked at them and sighed. Now I'm going to have two women soppy about New Zealand, he thought.

They stayed at a beautiful hotel right on the edge of the lake. Catherine and Mel enjoyed pottering round the shops. One sold beautiful hand-knitted woollen jumpers and cardigans, another sold black pearls and another opals, the latter mainly to Japanese tourists. There was a wide selection of cafes and restaurants and they went up in a gondola to the complex on top of a hill overlooking the lake and the mountains. Here they sipped champagne and were enthralled by the view.

'I think I've died and gone to heaven,' Mel murmured.

They went wine-tasting again, and of course Stuart continued his confrontation with New Zealand trout. As usual, the trout won!

Catherine and Mel were more than a little sad when they returned to Armidale. The hills and gum trees of home seemed just a little bit boring. Seeing a wistful expression on her father's face, Mel gave him a hug.

'Don't worry Daddy, I'll never leave you,' she promised.

'As long as you don't meet a handsome young Kiwi,' he joked.

'I promise I won't.'

Chapter 10

Mel couldn't wait to tell Emma all about her trip to New Zealand, the trip which was to substitute for not being allowed to go to schoolies week at Surfers Paradise. Mel also intended to let the trip stand in place of taking a gap year. Emma's family couldn't afford to send their daughter overseas, so she too forewent a gap year and Emma and Mel both decided to go straight to the University of New England to do a course in agricultural economics. Catherine was disappointed her daughter turned down their offer of a trip to Europe. She had fond memories of backpacking her way around Europe with two friends when she had left school. Moreover, she understood the girls wanted to start their university life together as both planning to get degrees in Agriculture Economics and then return to the family properties with fresh ideas and enthusiasm.

Before the university term commenced, Mel and Emma agreed to have a coffee in Armidale to discuss their new life and for Emma to suss out a few of the coffee shops with a view to getting a job which would help out her limited finances.

In January the streets of Armidale were unusually empty. There were no uni students, school students and only the odd tourist. Some stores were optimistically holding sales but there were few customers. In years gone by graziers coming to town with their wool cheques and cattle money had kept Armidale prosperous. By 2010, by now a city of 23,000, in it was more likely the numerous educational facilities that brought money to Armidale. There were the university, two private girl's schools, a private boy's school, a Roman Catholic high school, and two government-funded high schools as well a music conservatorium located in the Old Teacher's College. There were plenty of sporting facilities. The school boys played soccer, rugby league, and rugby union; and the girls played soccer, hockey and netball.

Mel and Emma were excited at the prospect of going to university after six confining years at boarding school. In Mel's little Honda, they drove out to the university in February in time for the start of orientation week. They had chosen to reside at Duval College, mainly because this was Catherine's college where she went to university.

The university had been founded in the 1938 when the White family made available their beautiful old home 'Boolaminbah' the beautiful old brick home, designed by the Hunt for the White family available. In the early years it was a college of Sydney University but after World War Two, buildings spread around Boolaminbah. These buildings were a mish-mash of architectural designs and shapes. This gave the university a higgledy-piggledy look of unplanned chaos. In 1954 it became a university in its own right, The University of New England, with a Chancellor and Vice-Chancellor who could deal with local problems by applying local solutions.

Mel and Emma left their luggage in their rooms at Duval College and set out to explore. In the corridor they ran into a couple looking slightly lost and confused. The girl was tall with long, straight, dark hair and her companion was a young man with a shock of brown hair, rumpled clothes and a slightly quirky expression. Both parties stopped. 'I'm Tina, short for Christine, and this is Tony,' the girl announced.

'Hi.' Tony added.

'Well, I'm Mel, short for Melanie.'

'And, I'm Emma and I'm just short.'

They all laughed, the ice had been broken.

'Have you got wheels?' Mel enquired.

'I've got an old bomb,' Tony answered. 'It's not pretty but it gets there.'

'If we're all going to have a look round we could all go together in my car,' Mel suggested.

'Thanks. That would be great.'

'Well, we're locals so we do know the layout, and you're both from …?'

'Sydney,' Tony and Tina answered together.

They all bundled into Mel's little Honda and made their way up Elm Avenue to the university campus proper. 'What courses are you doing?' Emma enquired.

'Rural Science.' Again they answered in unison.

'Cool, we're both doing Ag Economics. I think we do some of the same subjects in the first year,' Emma said.

Mel and Emma pointed out the buildings with which they were familiar. 'Bool', once the administration centre of the university, now housed a bar, bistro and restaurant. There were young people everywhere. Some wore shorts, tee-shirts and thongs, some of the girls, but not many, wore long dresses. They had short hair, long hair, spiky or coloured hair. Most of them looked bemused and some confused, others were grimly determined, marching from building to building trying to find the location of their particular subjects. Although the day was sunny, there was a chilly wind.

'I hope they brought their winter woollies,' Mel remarked of the students she observed. 'You never know when it's going to turn cold in this part of the world.'

Tina and Tony looked at each other. Winter woollies? What were they?

Mel and Emma wore jeans. Mel, because she never exposed more of her skin to the sun then she had to, and Emma because she thought shorts made her look too fat.

'We'll let you guys wander round and find your bearings. How about we meet back here in an hour?' Emma suggested.

'Ok, in an hour then,' Tina said

'That's cool,' Mel and Emma agreed.

When they had all arrived back at the college, they decided to spend the evening together at a designated pub. 'Each college has its pub,' Mel told them, 'and I suggest we all go together, then only one of us has to stay sober.'

'Then we'll take my car,' said Tony, 'and you three girls can drink as much as you like.'

They all laughed.

'We're not much of drinkers,' Mel explained, 'but I don't see why we can't celebrate our first day at uni.'

They had a bright and rowdy evening, exchanging life histories and meeting other students from their college. By eleven-o-clock, the girls were feeling more than a little sloshed. Tony of course was stone-cold sober after drinking squash all evening, so they decided to call it a night.

The rest of the week followed in much the same fashion, and then they had to get down to study, to lectures and the serious business of being a student at university.

After the first few days, Mel and Emma, having found out as much as they could about Tina and Tony, wondered what their relationship was.

'Do you think they're an item?' Emma asked.

'I don't think so,' Mel replied doubtfully. 'Tina says they're just friends.'

'Then how come they're doing the same course at the same university?'

'Gosh, I hope Tony is not gay!'

'I don't think he is.' Mel sounded a bit doubtful. 'No, I'm sure he's not,' she added.

'Of course you'd know,' Emma teased. 'You've had such a lot of experience with men.'

A few school-girl crushes was all the experience Mel had. 'Of course,' she replied in a superior voice, 'and you've absolutely none at all.'

Emma threw her hairbrush at her friend. 'I'm going to bed,' she said and left the room with great dignity.

It turned out that Tina Thomas and Tony Reede were next-door neighbours from Turramurra, one of the North Shore suburbs in Sydney. Their families had been friends as long as they could remember. Tina's father was a doctor, and Tony's a solicitor. Tony had an older brother who was following his father into the legal profession. He was five years older than Tony, and because Tony had a gap year, he had finished his degree and while Tony was going to university in Armidale, his brother Paul was joining his father's legal practice.

Tina's mother was fully engaged in working for charities. She was a member of quite a few organisations, not so much because she wanted to help the poor and needy but because she enjoyed mixing with the best people – the rich and well-connected. Tina's sister, Chloe, was a very pretty girl and a social butterfly, who flitted from party to party, dating the most eligible bachelors she could find in the hopes of making a 'successful' marriage.

Both Chloe and Tina had gone to Abbotsleigh in Wahroonga, which had a reputation for academic excellence, but many of the girls who attended it were also the daughters of the rich and famous. Tina was sickened by the superficial attitude to life of her mother and of her sister, both of whom depended on the father to work all hours to make enough money to fund his wife's and daughter's extravagant lifestyle. Tina had made friends at Abbotsleigh who were more interested in the environment, climate change, economic sustainability and equally weighty subjects.

Tina and Tony had long discussions about how they would like to get away from the city and live a less selfish life. Tony was also unimpressed by his father and brother's desire to make money at whatever the outcome for their clients. It was after many hours of talks, enquiries, discussions about their futures; Tony and Tina decided on Rural Science at UNE. Spurred on by the fact that his mother wanted him to marry, he was determined not to, and together with the fact that Tina just wanted to get away from Sydney, they both to set off for Armidale. They were certainly not an 'item' as Emma suggested, more like brother and sister, and each had great expectations for the years ahead.

It was the freedom that was exhilarating; the freedom to do what you wanted, when you wanted, or not to do anything at all. No teachers with strict rules, no disapproving parents. It was all so heady that some of the new students partied all night and slept all day, giving no thought to the real reason they were at university – to gain an education that would lead to good jobs and a promising future.

Mel and Emma both knew they had to work hard to justify their families' faith in their abilities, so that one day they could take over the running of their properties.

Tony was interested in water conservation, a big problem in Australia's drought and flood cycle. He was a clever and thoughtful young man and would have no problem in completing assignments or passing exams. Tina was more interested in renewable energy, hoping the world could move away from its dependence on oil, towards more eco-friendly alternatives.

Halfway through the first semester, Mel took her friends to visit Granny Rose. Rose knew Emma well from years of NEGS Grandparents' Days, Speech Days, and the like. Thus it was a tall elegant woman met them at the front door. Her hair was grey, she was beautifully groomed, wore an aqua linen skirt and shirt to match and pretty navy shoes.

'This is my Granny Rose,' Mel said to Tony and Tina.

Rose gave Emma a hug. Inside Rose enquired if they indulged in afternoon tea or would they prefer coffee or a cool drink.

'A cuppa would be lovely,' Mel exclaimed. The others agreed.

Rose provided not only tea but also some little cakes and pikelets with jam and cream. 'You are spoiling us,' Tina observed.

'I've always loved cooking,' Rose explained. 'Tell me, Emma, have you had any rain yet?'

Emma shook her head. 'I don't think it's ever going to rain again.'

'Just you wait, one of these days it will start raining, and after two or three years everybody will be saying – how I wish it would stop raining! You don't believe me? It will happen, I promise.'

They all settled down to work at the university but they were still left with plenty of time to play, and so the first semester passed swiftly.

One evening, the four sat having a drink at the pub when Mel asked Tony if he had any interests apart from his many and varied schemes for conserving water.

'Well, I do as a matter of fact. I nearly did a physics course instead of rural science,' he replied.

'You mean you're interested in Einstein's theory of relativity, and quantum mechanics and 'the big bang theory' and black holes and…'

Tony interrupted her. 'Dark matter, the 'string' theory?'

Mel sat up, her eyes shining. 'My Dad and I have great old talks about the universe and how it began and how it's slowly drifting apart. Tony, you would get on so well with Dad. We read all the books we find about it.'

Emma and Tina looked slightly bemused, but didn't interrupt.

'I know,' exclaimed Mel, 'You must all come home for the weekend. I think you'd get on famously with my parents.'

'It's a bit much to ask your mother,' Tina demurred.

'Of course not. She'd love it, she loves having visitors,' Mel said. 'She's always having lunch and dinner parties. They'd both love to meet you.'

Of course, Mel's parents already knew Emma from her years at NEGS. And so it was arranged for the following weekend.

'You know my father will love having someone to talk to on subjects that don't include the drought and how bad things are on the land, and my mother just loves cooking. She'll enjoy every minute.' Mel told Emma, confident it would prove be a great weekend.

Tony and Tina followed Mel and Emma in Tony's beat-up old car. They drove northeast out of Armidale on the Rockvale Road, then joined the Guyra-Ebor Road. It was slow going as Mel didn't want to lose Tony and on the gravel stretch through Rockvale, he had to stay back out of Mel's dust.

They finally reached Glenfoyle and were greeted warmly by Catherine and Stuart. After settling their gear in the various spare bedrooms, they settled in the lounge room to have a drink before dinner.

'This is a lovely house,' Tina congratulated Catherine, 'I love all your colour schemes.'

'Thank you, dear,' Catherine beamed.

'Don't mention colour schemes,' Stuart groaned, 'Once Catherine gets an idea, there's no stopping her, and the whole thing has to be redone from one end to the other.'

Mel giggled, remembering some of her mother's way-out colour schemes. 'I can remember when the kitchen cupboards were black, lime green and watermelon pink.'

Catherine flushed, 'Well, I'm going to check on the dinner in my beautiful blue and white kitchen.'

Tina felt a bit anxious. She hoped they hadn't offended Catherine.

'Can I do anything to help?' she offered.

'I'm fine, thank you,' was the reply.

'I must say you have a lovely view,' Tony commented to Stuart.

'Well, that was one of the reasons the house was built here, plus the fact that there is a nearby spring which has never been known to run dry. That's very important in this part of the world, a permanent water supply.'

He and Tony were soon in deep conversation, and Mel smiled happily. Things were going well.

'Your mother has some beautiful things,' said Tina, as she wandered around the room looking at the collections of ruby glass, Worcester and Doulton porcelain, and water colour paintings.

'Oh, you mean, stuff,' Mel laughed, knowing her mother's delight in collecting things.

'It's not stuff,' Tina replied. 'Your mother has very good taste.'

After a delicious baked dinner followed by an equally delicious berry crumble, Mel brought up the subject of black holes, and Stuart and Tony enthusiastically started a conversation which lasted for some time.

Next morning, Mel rose and wandered out the front, sat on her favourite rock, taking in the view, the sounds of the bush and the peace of it all. There were steps behind her. It was Tony. He found another rock to perch on. 'So this all belongs to your family?' he said wistfully.

'Well, about six miles where the country drops a couple of thousand feet. The hills you can see in the distance are on the northern side of the gulf country. If you climb to the top of the hill behind our house, you can see as far as Queensland, or so they say.'

'Really?'

'Well, I don't know really, it's just what people say.'

'And this will all be yours one day?'

'Yes, one day. I'm really looking forward to coming home and helping Dad.'

'You are lucky, Mel.

'Well lucky in everything except my fair colouring,' Mel answered ruefully. 'I have to wear jeans, long-sleeved shirts, big hats, and slap masses of blockout on my face and hands.'

'But you have beautiful colouring,' Tony asserted.

Mel laughed. 'It might be beautiful if you lived in the north of Scotland, but not in sunny old Australia.'

'Mel, Tony, where are you? Breakfasts ready,' Catherine called.

Obediently Mel and Tony made their way to the kitchen.

'Would you like to come for a drive round the place?' Stuart offered.

'Yes please, of course.'

'We've been lucky,' Stuart explained as they drove around the paddocks. 'In all these years of drought, we've still had some rain and good seasons. Not like poor old Em here,' he added.

'You can say that again,' Emma added. 'Our place is as dry as chips. We've been hand-feeding for years, and selling off a lot of our stock.'

'Years ago,' Stuart went on, 'we had so much feed we used to harvest it, and bury it in the pits for silage. We started breeding Santa Gertrudis cattle because Herefords were so prone to bloat. In my father's day he spent years clearing paddocks with dozers and tractors. Then they burnt the heaps of wood, planted pastures which were sown from the air. This gave us the opportunity to get through our cold winters without having to buy feed. But the last ten years have been so dry we are forced to buy feed, lucerne mostly but we also use lupins.'

To Emma's eyes the cattle looked fat and healthy and the sheep equally thriving. It nearly made her cry. Mel squeezed her friend's hand.

'It'll rain again one day,' she whispered.

'Things have changed so much,' Stuart continued. 'Now there are so many rules and regulations and extra paperwork, running a property is a different ball game. You can't get rid of one tree let alone clear a whole paddock.'

Stuart's father and grandfather had always treated their land with respect. They left belts of shelter in each paddock. Spreading superphosphate had improved their pastures and overall supering was ideal for some of their hilly and inaccessible country.

When Stuart was young all the mustering and stock work was done on horseback, which could be slow and time consuming. Motorbikes had changed all that, but Stuart had as many falls from bikes as he had from horses. The four-wheel bike was even more dangerous and there had been quite a few fatalities with these. Stuart would not let Mel ride a 'quad bike', as they were called.

On the whole it was a very successful weekend. 'You have a beautiful home,' Tina remarked to Mel a few days later. Secretly, she had been surprised by the obvious sophistication of Mel's parent's home.

'Did you think we were country bumpkins living in a humpy?' Mel laughed.

'Of course not,' Tina was a little offended. 'I really had no idea,' her voice trailed away.

'It's okay, Tina, I'm only teasing.' Mel didn't want to hurt her friend's feelings. 'Actually, it was pretty primitive living in the bush years ago in my grandparent's time – and great-grandparents. You know, no electricity, that sort of thing.'

'Sounds awful,' Tina ventured.

'When my Mum and Dad got married, because the mains electricity had been connected they were able to have all the mod-cons. But when my grandparents were married, the electricity was provided by a thirty-two volt engine that sat with the vehicles in a large shed at the back of the house. Her father had to run the engine every day so they could have lights. They bought special electrical appliances and they had to have a kerosene refrigerator. My grandmother hated it, if you had the flame too high everything in the fridge froze, too low and everything got too hot. Rose hated it. She always thought it would blow up. At least they had a septic system and an inside toilet.' Mel went on, 'They were really self -sufficient. Granddad milked a cow every day. They had chooks, grew their own vegies and fruit, and of course killed their own meat. Which we still do. Having freezers changed our life a lot. We have lamb in the summer and beef in the winter. In the old days they used to salt most of the beef to keep it, now it's just put in the freezer. Well, that's enough of my life history,' Mel laughed.

'It's jolly interesting.' Tina was impressed. 'People in the city have no idea what country life is like.'

'I agree with you there,' Mel commented. 'They just think we sit around waiting for the wool to grow, and raping the land in the process.'

'I liked your friends,' Catherine told her daughter the next time they spoke on the phone. 'Tony seems a very nice young man,' she added.

'Calm down, Mum, we're just friends,' Mel said.

'Your father liked him too,' Catherine added.

'Well, he is nice, and he's also very intelligent. I have lots of nice friends,' Mel added.

Catherine sighed. 'I didn't mean anything ...'

'Of course not, Mum. Take care,' Mel said airily and hung up.

She did like Tony and she loved talking to him. He had such a bright, enquiring mind but plenty of commonsense as well. But there was no spark between them, they were really just good friends. Apart from having drinks at the pub, the four of them would often get together in one of their rooms and talk into the small hours. Sometimes there were three, sometimes only two. Any subject was attacked with enthusiasm, chewed over, solved, left unsolved, and seen from every point of view.

Mel and Tony could talk for hours about the universe. Were there parallel universes? If the universe was created by the 'big bang', where did God come into it? Was there a God? If God created the universe, who created God? Why did God have to be a man – 'Our Father'? Didn't the human race need a mother more than a father? After all it was women who did most of the caring and nurturing in the home, so why couldn't we pray to 'Our Mother'. Then there was the notion that God was just an imaginary friend. But wasn't an imaginary friend better than no friend at all?

Tony waxed long and eloquently about Australia's water problems. After ten years of drought in New South Wales, he didn't think any government had really tackled the problem. Tina was more interested in a sustainable lifestyle. 'We should use less electricity, oil was obviously going to run dry one day. There should be better solutions to these problems.'

Climate change was a hot subject for conversation. Was it man-made or just the usual cycle of heat and cold the earth had been going through for millions of years?

Emma was mainly concerned about the drought and how it had affected her family so badly. Each of them felt they had to contribute in the best way they could to make the world a better place in which to live. But how? Why there was so much poverty, so much hate, so little compassion? Mel sometimes felt their talks were of more benefit to her than the lectures and assignments of her university course.

The weeks and months passed quickly and soon they were cramming for their exams.

'You're so cool, calm and collected,' Emma complained to Mel. 'I get all churned up when I think of exams.'

'Well, I'll be glad when they're over,' Mel agreed, 'but do you think we'll have passed the parents' exams?'

'What do you mean?'

'Alcohol, drugs and sex of course!'

Emma giggled. 'Well, we definitely didn't pass alcohol.'

'No, when I think of all the beers we've consumed ...' Mel laughed.

'And the odd tequila.'

'And the odd gin and tonic.'

'And the odd brandy.' They both laughed.

'I think we passed drugs,' Mel said.

'Definitely,' Emma said.

The drug issue had been easy for each of them. Mel didn't like the feeling that she wasn't in control and Emma simply couldn't afford them. 'And sex?' Mel asked pointedly

At an earlier stage Mel had decided she and Emma should do something about their sex lives, which were non-existent. 'Let's go to the pub and have a few drinks and see what happens,' she suggested. 'A few too many drinks.'

'Yes, a few too many drinks,' Emma said.

They were at the pub for a while and were getting more than slightly sloshed. Everything Mel said made Emma giggle helplessly but none of the young men seemed interested.

'This isn't working,' Mel whispered.

'Then we'll have to try a bit harder,' Emma replied.

Mel was ordering two more of the drinks they had been consuming just as Tony appeared behind them. He looked at the girls with disapproval. 'Are you girls getting drunk for any particular reason?' he asked.

Mel and Emma giggled helplessly.

'Tony, don't be such a grumble bum, we're just enjoying ourselves,' Mel explained.

'Well, I'm taking you home,' he insisted.

'Spoil sport!' they chorused.

He took each of them by the arm and marched them out to his car. He left them casually in their rooms, 'I didn't think you two could be silly.'

Next morning they both had headaches and felt more than a little foolish. 'The plot that failed,' Mel commented.

'I'm rather glad it did.' Emma said. 'I wonder what would have happened if Tony hadn't turned up?'

'Nothing probably,' Mel said wistfully. 'I guess we're not very attractive.'

'How depressing.'

Mel sighed. 'I guess it's back to studying.'

'Wouldn't our mothers be pleased – if they ever got to hear about it?'

When exams were over, Mel and Emma said goodbye sadly to Tony and Tina.

'See you next year.' 'See you.'

Mel and Emma knew they would see each other during the holidays. 'I guess we failed the sex exam,' Emma said despondently.

'I guess,' Mel said.

Emma was silent for a few minutes. 'It's a pity Tony's such a gentleman. He would never …'

'No, never.'

2011 began hot and dry. It became one of the hottest summers Armidale had ever had. The drought still had most of New South Wales in its deadly grip.

The 'famous four' had passed their exams with ease. Tony had high distinction in all subjects, the others were happy with their distinctions and passes.

Together, they had decided to move out of college and share a flat in the coming year although was left to Mel and Emma to make arrangements. Because they needed four bedrooms, most of the flats in town were too small. They eventually found a cottage which had belonged to Mel's grandparents. Then they begged, borrowed and stole enough furniture to make it habitable. They were relieved when lectures started again as both had worked hard on their properties in the long hot summer. Emma had helped hand-feed the few sheep her family had left of the property. All their cattle had been sold. Mel also helped her father with hand-feeding but found working out in the heat exhausting.

'I think I should be living in the north of Scotland,' she complained to her mother.

'Well, you could always marry a nice Scottish laddie and move there,' Catherine suggested helpfully.

'And where do I meet a nice Scottish laddie?'

'In Scotland, of course!' Catherine laughed.

It was great seeing Tony and Tina again and after catching up they settled down to lectures and life in their slightly tumble-down cottage.

And then there was Alex Douglas.

The girls had noticed him the year before. He was tall, dark and handsome, and revved around on a motor bike. He had quite a reputation with the girls, but his relationships didn't last long.

'He's awesome.' Mel heard some friends discussing Alex.

He was completing a degree in accountancy and he planned, when he had finished, to return to Tenterfield and work in the stock and station agency run by his father. Somehow, he started joining the group at the pub but mostly he chatted to Tony and did not take much notice of the girls. He seemed to have a good sense of humour and kept Tony amused with stories about his beloved motorbike.

Tony couldn't understand why this guy had suddenly become friendly but when he saw him glancing at Mel when he thought no-one was watching, he realised why.

'Do you like Alex?' he carefully asked Mel.

She shrugged. 'He seems okay, I haven't really talked to him much.'

But the chance came. As the others had to leave early one night, Mel found herself sitting alone at the pub. 'Hello, gorgeous.' A voice that was deep and attractive.

She looked up, startled. 'Oh, hi, Alex.'

He chatted easily for a while, ordered them both another drink, then: 'You have such beautiful eyes. They really are green, aren't they?'

'Cat's eyes,' Mel laughed. 'That was what the girls at school said.'

'I'm sure they were jealous, that's all,' he said sympathetically.

'I don't think so,' she murmured.

'And I love your red hair, you must have Scottish ancestors.' He put his hand out to touch the dark red tresses. Instinctively, she drew back and he dropped his hand.

Ho hum, he thought, this one's going to be a bit hard to get.

'My grandmother had red hair,' Mel said stiffly.

Alex finished his drink and stood up. 'Guess I'd better be going. Can I give you a lift?'

'Thanks, but I have my car,' Mel replied.

'See you,' and he was gone.

Mel sat for a while feeling slightly embarrassed and confused. Alex had got too personal too quickly and she wasn't sure if she was complimented or insulted.

Alex continued to join the group at the pub from time to time. Now he included the girls in his conversation but did not single out Mel for attention. He wangled an invitation to Sunday night at the cottage. The group had started having an informal get-together on Sunday nights. Friends came and went as they pleased and brought their own grog. The girls provided the food which was simple and no fuss, or they ordered pizzas or Chinese.

Emma had recently started going out with Clive Rogers, a medical student from Tamworth. He was able only do two years of his course in Armidale and then would be required to go to Newcastle to complete the program, so there was no long-term plan in this friendship. Tina also found a friend in Shane Edwards; nothing serious, they just enjoyed each other's company.

Finally Alex made his move. 'Like to come for a ride on my trusty steed, Mel?'

'Oh, I don't know. I'm more used to four wheelers,' Mel replied.

'Go on Mel,' Emma encouraged. 'It'll be fun.'

'Okay,' Mel said reluctantly.

'I have an extra helmet, you'll be quite safe.'

Tony watched with some concern. He quite liked Alex but there was something about him he didn't trust. And Mel? Well, Mel was so innocent and vulnerable. Tony had loved her from the first moment he saw her, but he knew she just thought of him like a brother. It had been difficult keeping his real feelings from showing, so he had thrown himself more and more into his studies.

Alex went for a spin around Armidale with Mel hanging tightly onto his waist.

'Thanks, that was fun,' Mel said when it was over.

'Any time.' Alex leaned over and kissed her cheek. 'See you.'

Alex started invite Mel to have dinner, go to the pictures, watch the local cricket teams. They were soon being asked to functions as a couple but Alex was careful not to become too familiar. He would kiss Mel goodnight gently on the lips but never hinted he'd like to come in and spend the night.

'Slowly does it,' he kept saying to himself, for the prize was beautiful and infinitely desirable.

Mel was flattered but confused. His touch made her nerves tingle, but she still didn't know if she actually liked him.

He told her about his family. His great-grandfather, he said, had arrived in Tenterfield in the early nineteen-hundreds.

'That must have been hard,' Mel sympathised.

'Well, he must have been a tough old boy. He bought some land, got married, had a couple of kids.'

'How did your father end up as a stock and station agent?'

'My grandfather wasn't very keen on the land and he married into the family who owned the agency. So he sold the property and now I'm expected to carry on the family business.'

'Do you really want to?' Mel asked.

'Sure, it's cool.'

'You haven't any brothers or sisters?'

'No, I'm an only child.'

'So am I!' exclaimed Mel.

'Well, we have that much in common.'

Finally Mel asked Alex to come out to Glenfoyle to meet her parents.

'Awesome,' he agreed, 'I'll burn out on my bike and then I can leave quickly if your parents don't like me.'

'Silly,' Mel laughed.

The following Saturday Mel set out, with Alex riding his bike a little way behind her so that he wouldn't be riding in her dust.

He was charming with her parents, especially Catherine. He said the right things, did the right things. His manners were impeccable. He sympathised about the hot, dry summer, informing them that his family business wasn't doing too well either.

Mel changed for dinner, putting on a pretty green frock that matched the colour of her eyes. Alex, who had only seen her in her university jeans and long-sleeved shirts, was dazzled.

'You look beautiful, green eyes,' he whispered as they went into the dining room for one of Catherine's famous baked dinners.

'You mean, cat's eyes,' she whispered back.

The next day Stuart took Alex on the obligatory tour of the property, and after lunch Alex left before Mel to get back to Armidale.

'Well, what'd you think of him?' she asked her mother hesitantly.

'Well, he's very charming and good-looking,' Catherine answered.

Mel's heart sank. These were not necessarily attributes that would impress her mother.

'Is it serious?' Catherine asked.

'No, of course not, we just hang out a bit.' Her voice trailed away, and she went to her room to pack her things.

But Catherine had seen the way Alex looked at her daughter and knew that he was serious if Mel wasn't. Serious about one thing and one thing only!

Early the next morning, after Mel had returned to Armidale, Stuart was woken by Catherine moaning, groaning and shaking. He put his arms around her and held her tight. 'Hush Catherine, wake up, you're just having a bad dream.'

She was still moaning and tears flowed down her cheeks.

'Catherine, wake up, wake up, darling.'

Her eyes flew open, frightened and confused.

'Oh, Stuart, I've had a terrible dream.' She clung to him desperately.

'It's all right, it was just a dream. You're safe. You know I wouldn't let anything bad happen to you.'

She started to shiver. 'It's not me, it's Mel.'

'It was just a dream.' He comforted her. He was used to her bad dreams and knew that most times she couldn't even remember what they were about. Even so, he asked, 'What was it about?'

As usual Catherine had to acknowledge, 'I, I don't really know. It just frightened me'

'Well, would you like a cup of tea? Shall I turn the light on, and you can sit up, that might make you feel better.'

'No, Stuart, I'll be alright now.'

'Go back to sleep, I'm sorry I woke you.'

At breakfast, Catherine was still pale and troubled.

'Are you sure you can't remember what the dream was about?' Stuart asked.

'You know me, I often have bad dreams.' She was trying to make light of her night terror.

'Yes, but they don't often upset you so badly. You said something about Mel.'

'Well yes, it was something about Alex, but I can't really remember.' Her voice trailed away.

Stuart changed the subject thinking that the sooner she forgot all about it the better.

'There's just one thing,' Stuart said. 'I don't think you should mention that dream to Mel.'

'No, of course I won't.'

'I want you to promise, Catherine, not to tell Mel. If you try to criticise Alex because you had a dream you can't remember she'll think you're nutty and be keener on him than ever. Promise?'

'I promise,' she said reluctantly. But she wouldn't let it be. 'Stuart, you know I've had dreams that have come true.'

'Yes, dear,' he said patiently. 'And a lot that didn't come true.'

'Oh, I have feelings about people, and I'm usually right. Remember that fellow who wanted to paint our fence, and I said no? There was something evil about him. Then he was caught trying to attack a girl at Ebor.'

'I remember.'

'And the day I knew something was wrong and you came off your bike and broke your arm? What about the dream I had before Melanie was born? I dreamt we had a red-haired baby girl and after we lost our little boys I just knew we were supposed to have a daughter.'

'Yes, dear.'

'Mel's a bit like me. She has dreams and she knows things. When I rang to tell her Aunt Mary had died she said, "I know Mum".'

'Well, she doesn't seem to share your opinion of Alex.'

'She will,' Catherine said firmly.

There had been showers on and off since the beginning of the year, but no-one would admit that they thought the drought was breaking. These showers continued to missed the land around Bundarra, much to Emma's disgust. But then the rain came properly. It became more persistent. Despite of the bad frost and low temperatures –Armidale's lowest ever – the days were mostly cloudy and drizzly. By August the meteorologists were claiming *El Nino* had been replaced by *La Nina*, names that described the warmth of the currents in the Pacific Ocean. *El Nino* meant droughts and *La Nina* meant rain and even floods. It even rained in Bundarra in August and September.

The area that was drought declared in NSW shrank month by month. At last people began to believe perhaps the drought was over. Tractors were bogged, roads became slippery, Armidale shops sold a lot of umbrellas. Could this really be happening after the many dry and despairing years? Farmers smiled as they compared each other's rainfall readings. Yet again, Australia showed it had an extreme climate, from drought to flood – there was little in-between.

After battling through the recent Global Financial crisis and the drought, most people felt more optimistic and more cheerful; the floods were yet to come. The area had not had such a good spring for many years.

The only thing that worried Mel was the increasing coolness in her mother's attitude to Alex. The next time he came to visit Glenfoyle, the atmosphere was chilly.

'I don't think your mother likes me,' Alex complained to Mel when they had returned to Armidale.

'Don't be silly. She's just being an over-protective mother.'

But Mel too had noticed her mother's behaviour. She had tried to find out what was wrong, but Catherine brushed her daughter's questions aside. Her father had been his usual affable self and seemed to be over-compensating for Catherine's coldness. Mel had asked her father if anything was wrong.

'No, of course not. Don't worry, Mel. It's probably just your mother's age – you know.'

Well, thought Mel, I just wish Mum wasn't taking her menopausal feelings out on Alex.

Tony could see that Mel was worried. 'Is anything wrong between you and Alex? You do still like him?' he asked.

'What a silly question. I wouldn't go out with him if I didn't like him.' She thought for a moment; although Alex's love-making still excited her, she couldn't decide if she did really like him. She wasn't comfortable with him like she was with Tony, and she couldn't talk to him about everything like she did with Tony. Sometimes, Alex was light-hearted and good fun, at others he was silent and preoccupied. At these times, if she asked him if anything was wrong he would snap at her. Perhaps her mother knew something about him that Mel didn't know, but what could it be? She sighed.

'I don't know,' she admitted. 'Sometimes I like him and sometimes I don't.'

'Well, you know the old saying: If in doubt, don't,' Tony said enigmatically.

She quickly looked at him, trying to read his expression, but she couldn't. 'Well, I'll make up my own mind about it, thank you,' she said coldly. 'I'm going to do my assignment,' and she went to her room.

Damn, thought Tony, why did I say that? Damn! Damn! Damn!

At the end of the winter semester Mel invited Alex to come home with her for a few days before he went back to Tenterfield. She was hoping she would be able to ease her strained relations between her mother and her boyfriend.

Before they arrived, Stuart begged Catherine to be friendlier towards Alex. 'You must try,' he urged. 'You run the risk of losing your daughter if you go on with this disapproving attitude.'

'I'll try,' she promised.

The visit started off well, with Catherine making the effort to cook a beautiful meal, and even make polite conversation.

'You'll see, she'll come around. How would anyone not like you?' Mel teased Alex as they walked together after the meal.

He held her tight, feeling her soft young body pressed close to his. He was filled with an overwhelming desire to pick her up, carry her to the room where they could make mad, passionate love. He was beginning to think the long months of his attempts at gentle persuasion were not going to be rewarded. Why should he wait around for Mel's mother to give him her approval when he could have any other girl any time. But Mel was beautiful, she came from a wealthy family and he wanted her more than he had ever wanted another girl. Perhaps it was marriage and only marriage that 'darling mummy' wanted for Mel. He shuddered at the thought. They were both far too young to be married. They needed to finish their courses as university first.

Alex tossed and turned for most of the night, not knowing what he should do next.

Breakfast was a little strained. Catherine's pretended good humour was wearing a little thin. She hadn't slept much either, but she knew

Stuart was keeping a close eye on her, making sure she didn't start talking about dreams, remembered and unremembered.

'Let's go for a spin on Daisy,' Alex suggested to Mel.

'What a good idea.' Mel was grateful they could escape before her mother's mood deteriorated more.

'Don't be long,' Catherine admonished, a strange look on her face.

'Course not, we won't be long.' Dangerous words...

'I'd like to show you where my great-grandparents used to live,' Mel explained as they went out to the garage where Alex had left his bike. 'Not that there's anything left of their house, or their garden for that matter. But there's a beautiful old magnolia tree there. It must be a hundred years old, and I think it's the most beautiful tree in the world.'

The tree grew about a mile back along the road but not far from where Mel's grandparents had lived. As they drew close the tree could be seen, standing in magnificent solitude.

As he tried to get a little closer to the tree, Alex's front tyre hit a rock, a rock he hadn't noticed because he was looking at the magnolia tree. The bike lifted off the ground and landed on its side, throwing Mel and Alex in the air then on to the ground.

Painfully, Alex stood up. His arm was hurting like hell but Mel was still lying on the ground where she had fallen. 'Mel, Mel Are you all right?' She didn't stir.

Her helmet had been knocked off by the fall. 'Silly girl, she can't have put it on properly.'

As he leant over he realised to his horror that Mel wasn't breathing. Oh my God, what'll I do? CPR of course, CPR, but how do you do it? I've got to do it.

He pressed her chest with his hands and breathed into her mouth, absolute panic and fear drove him on. After a few seconds Mel gurgled, almost choked, then started breathing. Her eyes fluttered open.

'Wh... what happened?'

Alex was shaking from head to foot, and his whole body was trembling. 'We had a bit of a buster. Tell me, Mel, does anything hurt?'

'My head.'

'No, don't move it,' Alex warned. 'Nowhere else hurts? Good. Now wiggle your fingers and toes to see if they move. Good. Now I'm going to ring for an ambulance.'

By good fortune, his mobile phone survived the crash. Alex dialled 000 and told the emergency service what had happened and where they were. Then he rang Stuart.

It only took Stuart and Catherine a few minutes to arrive but to Alex it seemed like an eternity. He kept talking to Mel. 'Are you sure nothing else hurts? Your Mum and Dad will be here in a minute, and so will the ambulance.'

Catherine rushed to her daughter's side. 'Are you alright? Oh my darling, does anything hurt?'

'My head,' Mel repeated.

'Well, you just lie very still and the ambulance will be here soon,' Catherine said.

Alex stood up. 'She stopped breathing for a few minutes.' His voice was husky and he still shook.

'What...?' Catherine turned and stared at him.

'Luckily I remembered how to do CPR.'

'Good boy,' Stuart said.

Catherine looked closer at Alex. 'Alex, your arm, you've broken your arm.'

Alex looked down and saw his arm was a peculiar shape. 'I hadn't noticed,' he stammered.

'You mean you gave her CPR and didn't notice your arm was broken?' Stuart exclaimed

Alex shook his head, things started to spin around.

'I think you'd better come and sit in the car.'

When an air-ambulance arrived, Alex explained to the paramedics that Mel had stopped breathing and he had brought her round.

'By the look of your arm I think you'd better come with us too.' The paramedics made Mel comfortable, got her on a stretcher and into the chopper.

'We'll be at the hospital as soon as we can,' Stuart said to Alex

'Don't worry, we'll look after them,' one of the paramedics said. The helicopter sent up a great cloud of dust and then it and its passengers were gone.

By the time Stuart and Catherine reached the Armidale hospital, a doctor was with Mel and Alex had been taken to get his arm set. Stuart rang Granny Rose. 'One of us will stay with Mel overnight, while the other gets some sleep.'

'I'll make up a bed straight away, and I'll say some prayers for you all,' said Rose.

'Thanks, Mum,' Stuart said.

The doctor who had examined Mel seemed optimistic that she had suffered no serious long-term effects. 'Even so, we'll do some tests tomorrow to make sure everything is alright. You must be grateful to that young man of yours, he saved her life.'

'What?' Catherine looked at her husband as the doctor disappeared along the passage.

'Mel stopped breathing for a moment after the fall, but Alex brought her around with CPR,' Stuart said gently.

'Oh, Stuart.' She clung to him, appalled at how close they had come to losing their daughter.

They decided to take turns sitting with Mel during the night. Catherine stayed until midnight, after which Stuart sat with her until morning. Catherine arrived back at the hospital as Mel was waking. She had slept peacefully most of the night.

'How are you, darling?' Catherine asked.

'I feel fine but you two look dreadful,' Mel replied.

'Thanks a bunch,' her father joked.

'Oh, I'm sorry, I didn't mean… I know someone was here all night, you poor things you must be exhausted.'

'As long as you're okay, that's the main thing,' her father asserted.

'I feel fine, my head hurts a little that's all. Do you know how Alex is?'

'He stayed in overnight,' Catherine explained. 'I'm sure he'll be along to see you as soon as he can. We have a lot to thank him for.'

'He saved my life,' Mel whispered and her eyes filled with tears.

There were X-rays and other tests planned to make sure there was no damage inside her head, so Catherine and Stuart took the opportunity to have breakfast with Rose, have a shower, change their clothes and hope that Mel would be alright.

When Mel was back in her bed after having an MRI, Alex knocked on the door. 'Are you decent?' he asked.

'Of course I'm decent, you silly thing!'

He came, sat by the bed, held her hand with his good hand and tried to speak.

'What's the matter? Is your arm very painful?' Mel asked anxiously.

'No, it just hurts a bit. It's just that… Oh Mel, I'm sorry you were hurt.'

'It was just an accident. It wasn't your fault.'

'It was my fault. I should have been looking where I was going. I'm so sorry Mel I'm so sorry you were hurt. I couldn't bear it if anything, anything else had happened to you.' He stumbled over his words, shook his head then leant over and buried his head in the lovely red hair framing her face and tumbling over her pillow.

Mel gently stroked his head. 'It's alright, Alex. I'm all right, there's no need to be upset.'

Alex lifted his head. 'I am upset. I love you Mel, I love you so much and couldn't bear anything bad happening to you.'

She looked into his eyes, amazed and confused. Where was the cynical, hard drinking, flirtatious, selfish Alex that she had known? He kissed her gently on her soft delicious lips.

Mel was surprised to hear herself saying, 'I love you too, Alex.'

'Do you really?'

In the desperate moment when Alex had realised Mel wasn't breathing, he had changed from a tear-about to a thoughtful caring man. When Mel heard herself saying she loved Alex, she changed from girl to woman.

'Ah hum.' Stuart and Catherine came into the room.

'I think we're interrupting,' Catherine apologised.

Alex stood up, looking embarrassed. Mel flushed pink.

'How's your arm this morning, Alex?' Catherine enquired.

'A lot better, thank you, hardly hurts at all.'

The doctor returned later in the day with good news for the Harrisons. 'There doesn't appear to be any swelling in the brain, but I suggest Mel stay in a couple more nights, just for observation.' He turned to Mel, 'But I must impress on you, Mel, if you have any headaches at all, let me know straight away.'

Emma, Tony and Tina visited Mel in the hospital and assured her they would look after Alex while he was unable ride his bike.

'He can have your bed,' Emma suggested mischievously. 'We'll look after him,' she promised.

It was only a few weeks to their final exams, and Mel and Alex plunged back into studying.

The doctor told Mel to take the studying quietly for the first few days.

Granny Rose was impressed by Mel's boyfriend and most interested in his background.

Stuart was surprised by Catherine's change of heart. 'I thought you didn't like Alex?' he asked.

'Well, he did save Mel's life,' she explained.

'I'm surprised you didn't dream a happy ending for them, I thought you dreamt something terrible was going to happen.'

'Well it did,' Catherine replied impatiently, 'I can't dream every single thing that's going to happen.'

'What a pity,' Stuart teased. 'Would have saved yourself a lot of worry.'

Catherine ignored him.

Mel went back to university classes. Alex slept on the couch in the lounge room and the five of them studied hard. They were all so engrossed in their final examinations it took Emma to notice the change in the attitude between Mel and Alex. 'What's going on?' she asked.

'Nothing,' said Mel, airily and changed the subject.

Rose found an opportunity to have a discussion with Catherine about something that had been concerning her.

'Do you know much about Alex's background?' she asked.

'Well not really,' Catherine admitted. 'His family have been stock and station agents in Tenterfield for ages. I think they might have come from Sydney originally. In fact, I gather there is a story that one of his ancestors was a convict.'

This was of no consequence by the twenty-first century. In fact people were proud to have convict ancestors. Rose did not consider it important. 'You know how Mel likes to sit on the hill down the paddock where Demelza died?' she asked.

'Yes, and no-one ever told her and no-one ever will tell her about Demelza,' Catherine insisted

'Yes, yes but the neighbours at the time, they were Scottish, the McDougalls.' Rose said.

'Yes, I suppose so,' Catherine said, unsure of where this was going.

'And the lad who was accused of causing the accident was Alexander McDougall?'

'So it was said but it wasn't true, a snake spooked Demelza's horse.'

'Well, even going further back to the Gregory family when they lived at Melrose Park in England. Amelia Gregory had a fall and a young Scottish boy was accused of attacking her.'

'But Rose, you know that wasn't true either. He claimed he had never touched Amelia, and he went back to Scotland, or so everyone thought.'

'I know now his name was Alexander McDougall and he was transported to New South Wales as a convict the same year Amelia had her accident,' Rose said.

A realisation at what Rose was saying starting to dawn in Catherine's mind. 'But Amelia did not die from the fall,' she said.

'No, but her mother claimed it was the bump on her head that was the reason she died when Milly was born,' Rose said.

'And now you are saying that years later his grandson lived next door to Demelza and her family. But what has that got to do with Alex Douglas?'

'I've taken it on myself to go into Alex's family tree, and there is a dead end. And the year Demelza died, the McDougalls from Brookdale just seemed to disappear. Perhaps the Alec McDougall changed his name to Douglas.'

Rose and Catherine were silent and thoughtful. Finally Catherine said what was on both their minds. 'They must never know.'

'We must never tell them,' Rose agreed.

'It would haunt them.'

'It's haunting me. I kind of wish I'd never connected it all up,' Rose said. 'That a Scottish boy and a girl with red hair have loved each other for two hundred years?'

'We must let them work their own lives out, and hope they never find out,' Catherine said. 'The present and the future are difficult enough to cope with, without being weighed down by two hundred years of tragedies, lost opportunities and heartbreak.'

'They are a fine young couple and we must support them as best we can, with whatever they want to do.'

At last the exams were over. Tina and Tony said goodbye to Mel and Emma. Of course Mel would see Emma over the holidays. It was only Alex was not coming back. Next year he would be working for his father in the family stock and station agency.

Alex called at Glenfoyle to stay the weekend before he returned to Tenterfield. When he arrived, he couldn't find Mel. 'Mrs Harrison, do you know where Mel is?'

'Well, if she's not in the garden she could be down the hill. She has a favourite spot she likes to sit and admire the view.'

'Thanks, Mrs Harrison. I'll go and have a look around.'

There Mel was, lying back in the grass, looking at the clouds. Alex sat down beside her and took her hand.

'Do you think you can really see as far as Queensland?' he asked.

'Of course you can. You can see anything if you really want to.'

They turned and looked at each other. They looked deep into each other's eyes, into each other's souls, down the minutes, months, years, and they smiled. It seemed that suddenly everything was all right with the world. It was spinning through space on its allotted course just as Mel and Alex were about to set out on their allotted course.

'Yes, oh yes please,' was her answer.

Epilogue

Rose invited her next-door neighbour Helen to come and meet the newest member of the family. As usual, Rose provided a tasty afternoon tea for the family who had gathered in her living room and when they heard a baby cry all present turned to see Mel entering the living room with a baby in her arms.

'Isn't he beautiful?' Helen gazed at the baby. 'What have you called him?'

'He's Allen Alexander Douglas,' Mel explained proudly. 'Allen after his great-great-great-great-grandfather, so we know he'll be brave, Alexander after his father, so he'll be handsome and charming. Best of all he has red hair like mine.'

'He's just beautiful,' Helen cooed, 'and such unusual colouring, red hair and brown eyes.'

'Usually the girls in my family have red hair,' Mel went on with a quick look at her husband, 'but Alex and I decided to change all that.'

'You mean you can choose the sex and colouring of your baby?' Helen was astonished.

'No dear,' Rose patted her friend's arm, 'Mel was just joking.'

'Oh well, of course,' Helen stood up feeling confused and embarrassed. 'Thank you so much, I've had a lovely afternoon, must get home, things to do.'

Rose accompanied her to the door. When she returned to the family room, Catherine was cuddling the baby and Mel and Alex were cuddling each other and smiling.

A mischievous smile or a knowing smile? Rose didn't know.

'Can any dream come true?' Rose wondered.

Acknowledgements

I would like to thank my daughter Katrina for arranging to have my manuscript typed, my daughter Kirstie for her support in the daily problems caused by my failing eyesight, my son Tim for his encouragement and help with some of the necessary research and my friends Jean Evans and Jackie Lamble for also helping to research aspects of the life of captain Allen Gardiner.

About the Author

Janet Robertson was born in New Zealand and moved in 1947, with her family, to Armidale, New South Wales. She married soon after leaving school and lived on a property in the Australian bush for forty-four years. Upon retirement to Armidale and despite failing eyesight she continued the painting and writing she had done for some years. With determination and perseverance, she completed this book in 2012 even though she knew she would not be able to read it.